HOW to (ALMOST) RUIN YOUR SUMMER

TARYN SOUDERS

sourcebooks
jabberwocky

Published by Sourcebooks Jabberwocky, an imprint of Sourcebooks, Inc.
P.O. Box 4410, Naperville, Illinois 60567-4410
(630) 961-3900
Fax: (630) 961-2168
www.sourcebooks.com

Library of Congress Cataloging-in-Publication data is on file with the publisher.

Source of Production: Versa Press, East Peoria, Illinois, USA
Date of Production: April 2016
Run Number: 5006447

Printed and bound in the United States of America.
VP 10 9 8 7 6 5 4 3 2 1

To my husband, David, and Charlie the Bear

Friday, June 11
Start Off with a Plan

. . . .

SOMEONE ONCE TOLD ME that money can't buy happiness. They obviously never had to ride a baby bike to the first day of middle school.

My parents didn't think there was anything *wrong* with my existing bike, so they weren't going to shell out money for a new one before school started in the fall. Apparently they didn't realize that in middle school, once you've been labeled a "dork," you're stuck with that label. *My* dorkiness would come in the form of a hot-pink bicycle plastered with Dora the Explorer stickers. Definitely not a stellar way to debut my sixth-grade year. But the parents said if I wanted a new bike, I'd have to pay for it myself. And of course, the bike I had my heart set on, an Alpine Traverse, cost $385.00.

My best friends, Elenna and Jireh, didn't need new bikes, but they were obsessed with the idea of getting Zoo 'n' Yous. I couldn't turn on the TV without seeing a commercial of giggling girls at a slumber party wrapped up in oversized blanket-pillow combinations that looked like animals. The pillow part of a Zoo 'n' You was shaped like an animal's head, and the attached blanket looked like fur. It even had sleeves to slip your arms into, so you could wear it like a robe—if you wanted the pillow hanging down your back. Personally, I found the whole concept bizarre and could think of a million other ways to spend $49.99 plus shipping and handling.

Either way, Elenna, Jireh, and I all needed money. The only way we could think to earn it was babysitting. The library offered a free babysitting class at the beginning of each summer. They taught CPR and everything, and the three of us had signed up right away.

My plan for summer was simple: make lots of money to buy a new bike.

That was it.

Nothing else.

No summer school. No road trips. No awkward family reunions.

And definitely no camps on account of I'd heard they have tons of spiders. (I'm absolutely terrified of anything with eight legs. Actually, anything with more than two and you're asking for trouble. Animals are irritating, destructive, and smelly. And the problems snowball the more legs they have. By the time you get to eight, watch out world!)

My parent's plan, on the other hand, was to celebrate their fifteenth wedding anniversary by taking a two-week-long Alaskan cruise...alone.

They came into my bedroom one night while I was reading and handed me a letter.

Dear Chloe McCorkle,

Let me be the first to say we are looking forward to having you at Camp Minnehaha. Enclosed you will find a packing guide and other helpful information. Please take the time to read through the electives we offer and get ready for two weeks filled with fun and excitement!

Sincerely,

Linda Mudwimple
Camp Director

My jaw dropped as my eyes darted back and forth between my parents and the letter.

"Umm...I have other plans." I folded the letter and held it out to my mom.

Mom smiled.

Dad barked a laugh so loud I dropped the letter. Based on their responses, strategic negotiating was needed if I wanted to get my way. I could handle this like an adult—after all, I *was* going into middle school. I decided to use last year's lessons in Peer Mediation about handling conflict. I needed to A.C.T.

- Acknowledge the other person's feelings.
- Compliment them.
- Thank them.

I cleared my throat. "I get that you're going on a cruise, and I need to be somewhere while you enjoy Arctic blasts of air and whale watching. This Camp Minnehaha, while I'm sure it's fascinating, doesn't really fit into my summer plans. Thanks for thinking of me though."

Nailed it.

Mom raised one eyebrow and smiled with one side of her mouth—a look that directly translated to *Think again.*

Maybe reasoning would work.

"But now I'll never be able to get a new bike!"

"The bike you have is perfectly fine," Dad said.

"It's adorable!" Mom added.

Yeah—adorable if you're a DORK.

I tried reasoning again. "I would really like to take the babysitting class at the library with Elenna and Jireh. I can't do that if I'm not here."

"The library offers the class more than once, Chloe," Dad said. "You can take the babysitting class when you return."

It was time to resort to begging—it wasn't very adult-like, but it sometimes worked. I clasped my hands together in desperation. "But Elenna and Jireh are taking the *first* class," I whined. "Those two will get all the babysitting jobs for the summer."

Dad pulled a brochure from his shirt pocket and handed it to me.

I slowly took it from him and then read aloud, "Camp Minnehaha is a fun, educational, kid-approved career camp, surrounded by gently rolling hills and clear streams." I narrowed my eyes and cocked a brow. "What's a career camp?"

Dad tapped the brochure. "It's where you'll see what it's like to be a cake decorator, athlete, scientist, and veterinarian," he said. "You try them all out the first week, and the second week, you pick your favorite and spend the rest of the time exploring that career in depth."

"Sounds thrilling," I said. "You know animals and I

don't get along and you want me to spend time pretending to be a veterinarian?"

When I was nine, my parents got me a hamster that I named What (because he always had an expression on his face like he was asking a question). Every time I picked him up, he'd pee on me and then bite my finger. After six months, he escaped from his cage and was never seen again. I couldn't even keep a hamster safe and healthy. I didn't need to go to some career camp to know I'd never be a vet.

This was horrible! It wasn't just the fact that going off to camp meant I couldn't hang with Elenna or Jireh. It also meant that when middle school started in the fall, I was going to be riding my baby bike. Put that together with my terrible hair problem, and I was going to be looking like the World's Biggest Dork.

My hair? Totally out of control. On a good day, I looked like an electrocuted lion. And if the humidity was extra high, I could be mistaken for Medusa. Mom always said I was beautiful, but moms are supposed to say nice things.

My hair I couldn't change, but my bike situation I could…or at least I had hoped.

Dad looked at me sadly and moved toward my door. A dagger of guilt poked my conscience. I knew they signed me up for camp thinking I'd enjoy it. I hated disappointing them.

I glanced at the brochure. "Cake decorating, huh?" Ever since the show *The Baker's Dozen* aired on TV, I'd obsessed over every episode. Thirteen people would compete in decorating cupcakes for $5,000.

Mom joined Dad near my bedroom door, signaling the end of the family meeting. "Get some sleep, sweetie. In the morning, we'll go shopping for the things you'll need. You leave the day after tomorrow." She winked. "I'm so excited for you!"

I flipped through the camp brochure and paused at the "Cake Decorating" page.

A few weeks ago my friend Mrs. Peghiny, the owner of Peghiny's Ice Cream Parlor, had introduced her new ice cream flavor, Cupcake Confetti. She told me she also wanted to sell cupcakes at the parlor since the ice cream was sooooo popular. The only thing stopping her was she didn't have time.

A brilliant idea popped into my head. My forced exile to Camp Minnehaha just might work in my favor—as long as Mrs. Peghiny agreed to my plan.

Saturday, June 12
Leave Mr. Snuffles at Home

. . . .

SATURDAY AFTERNOON, MOM AND I returned home with bags loaded with sunscreen, Bug-Me-Not, a flashlight, a ton of batteries, and every hair product that came in travel size.

As I laid my camp things on my bed to label them, Mom came in holding a turquoise leather-bound journal with silver-sequined dragonflies. She grinned and handed it to me. "I noticed you kept picking this up when we were at Murphy's Attic, so I bought it when you weren't looking."

I took it from her. "Cool. Thanks."

"You can use it to express your feelings. It will help you process things about separation anxiety or worries about middle school."

Oh brother.

Processing emotions was a mega-big deal to Mom. Last week, she sat Jireh, Elenna, and me down for what she called a "here and now" to tell us it was healthy and normal to openly express our emotions. She'd overheard a small part of a conversation we'd had in the backyard. I'd said that "bottled" was the way to go, and they had both agreed. After the therapy session she put us through about how we shouldn't keep our feelings bottled up, she concluded with her usual lecture on hormones. I explained we were simply talking about canned sodas versus bottled sodas and which tasted better.

How awkward was that?

I touched one of the dragonflies on the cover of the journal, wondering how it would hold up shoved into my suitcase. "Do you think I should I take it to camp?"

"Absolutely!"

We were about to start packing when Dad hollered something from the kitchen about the dishwasher spewing soap.

Mom rushed out the door.

As I plopped my suitcase on the bed and flipped it open, I glanced at the clock on my desk. If I hurried, I'd have plenty of time before dinner and after packing to make it down to Peghiny's Ice Cream Parlor.

I'd never packed for camp before, and the more items I placed into my suitcase, the faster my heart pounded. I'd been to sleepovers millions of times, but this was completely different.

I glanced at Mr. Snuffles, who was on my bed. I named him Mr. Snuffles after my favorite *Sesame Street* character, Mr. Snuffleupagus. He was a small, gray elephant who wore a T-shirt that said *Someone in Colorado Loves Me.* In his trunk, he held a red rose. My grandpa had given him to me for my third birthday, and he'd quickly become a favorite. After Grandpa died two years ago, I had treasured Mr. Snuffles even more.

Unfortunately, he no longer *looked* like a treasure.

He was dingy—even for a gray elephant. His head flopped to one side because no stuffing was left in his neck. Several places on his body were so worn that wisps of stuffing poked out. His T-shirt was ragged and sported spaghetti sauce stains from when I used to set him next to me at the dinner table. His eyes didn't even match. One of them had fallen off a long time ago, and Mom had sewed on a button to replace it—only it didn't look like the other eye at all.

Even though I loved him, he wasn't getting into my suitcase. I'd rather eat a full pan of Mom's meatloaf (which was gross) than be caught with Mr. Snuffles at camp.

He sat there, looking at me. His mismatched eyes seemed to be pleading, begging to come with me.

"I am not bringing you," I told him. "Everyone will think I'm a baby."

I tossed him onto my beanbag chair and threw a pillow over him. I didn't need a guilt trip from Mr. Snuffles.

Ten minutes later, I set my packed suitcase and sleeping bag next to my dresser.

Clothes—check.

Shower junk and hair-taming goops and gels—check.

No babyish stuffed animals—check.

Mom poked her head into my room. A blob of suds rested on the top of her head like a small tiara. "Dishwasher's on the fritz. The kitchen floor is covered in soap! Gonna grab more towels but wanted to check—" She stopped and raised an eyebrow at the sight of the packed suitcase.

"You seemed pretty busy, what with the dishwasher spewing bubbles, so I figured I'd go ahead and pack." I plopped into my beanbag chair (sitting on Mr. Snuffles), clasped my hands behind my head, and crossed my ankles. "It's all good. I used the list—and if I forgot anything, y'all can just turn the cruise ship around and bring it to me."

She smirked. "Ha-ha."

"Can I bike down to the ice cream parlor real quick? I want to say good-bye to Mrs. Peghiny."

Dad hollered again, and Mom glanced down the hall. "Be back in time for dinner—and don't fill up on a lot of ice cream."

After dinner that night, I pulled the new journal from my suitcase. I'd never had one before and I wasn't sure how to start "expressing myself."

Dear Diary,

Dear Journal,

Dear Paper Shrink,

In the end, I decided to just stick with the date and time.

Saturday, June 12
8:56 p.m.

Mom got me this journal to "process feelings." I think she feels guilty for sending me off to camp.

Mom and Dad are making me go to Camp Minnehaha for two weeks while they go on a cruise. I am not about to let their Arctic adventure ruin my summer though.

I came up with a NEW plan!

PLAN B.

This afternoon, I told Mrs. Peghiny about the cake decorating class at Camp Minnehaha. I suggested she could pay me to decorate her cupcakes—'cause I would be like a REAL cake decorator after camp. It took a little bit of convincing, but in the end, she said that if I took the class and did well, she'd try me out as her cupcake decorator! I bet I could even compete on *Baker's Dozen* after going to camp!

Plus, it will be way better than babysitting, duh!

Speaking of fun, Mom and Dad think the camp will be fun...which is what adults always say when they actually have no idea what's going to happen.

I've hidden Mr. Snuffles—I'll really miss him, but I can't bring him. Because the only thing worse than MISSING Mr. Snuffles would be the way all the kids would laugh at me if they saw him!

Sunday, June 13
Watch Your Parents Drive Away

. . . .

ON THE LONG DRIVE to camp, I told Mom and Dad about my moneymaking plan. Dad said it was a good idea, and Mom said she liked the fact I was focusing on positive outcomes (she's always saying stuff like that).

"We're here," Dad said.

We turned off the county road onto a gravel drive and passed under a huge *Welcome to Camp Minn haha* sign. The fact that the *e* was missing and the sign now ended with "haha" was not encouraging.

The parking lot swarmed with boys and girls who looked my age or close to it, tugging and lugging suitcases and sleeping bags. Dad parked, and I dragged myself from the van to stretch my cramped muscles.

The scent of pine trees and sunscreen filled my nostrils. "I bet this is what Christmas in the tropics smells like." Then, a breeze brought the stench of sawdust and manure to us—what summer camp with barn animals smells like.

My mother spoke under her breath. "Oh my."

That didn't make me feel any better.

Where were the clear streams and the gently rolling hills? All around me were what looked like mountains. The mere thought of hiking up and down them made my legs ache. But Camp Minnehaha was my ticket to non-dorkiness. *Stay focused, Chloe!*

At the top step of the registration office—actually it said *Reg st ation Off ce*—perched a woman just under five feet tall and just over three feet wide. She greeted the campers and parents grouping near her. "Welcome, welcome, welcome! Hello, hello, hello!" She could give Mrs. Claus a run for her money when it came to both size and cheeriness. Dressed in khaki from head to toe, she looked prepared to go on safari. Wire-rimmed glasses balanced on the tip of her nose. "I'm Director Mudwimple."

She barreled down the three rickety steps toward us, amazingly fast for someone her size. I hoped she wouldn't gain too much speed and run into me. She grabbed my hand and shook it in a two-handed, crushing grip before she moved onto the next person in her path, talking nonstop. "If you have any medications, just leave them in the nurse's office. Also, you'll need to fill out some medical forms, waivers, that sort of thing. The registration office is just behind me, and they'll give you your cabin assignments, career information sheets, and the daily schedule. Orientation is at three o'clock, and here is a map of the camp." She'd circled back around to where I stood, shoved a map into my hands, and took a deep breath before starting in again on her well-rehearsed welcome speech. I couldn't listen as fast as she could talk.

Despite the shade of the pine trees, the afternoon sun toasted me like a marshmallow. Wavy lines of heat rose from the tops of cars, and beads of sweat trickled down my back. I wriggled my shoulders in irritation. Folding the map Director Mudwimple gave me into a fan, I waved the tropical Christmas–smelly barn breeze toward my face, and we walked inside the *Reg st ation Off ce*.

A ginormous stone fireplace stood in the center of the air-conditioned room. Couches and armchairs were scattered around in small groupings, like tiny living rooms all set up in one giant space. Kind of like pictures of log cabins I'd seen in Mom's home-decorating magazines. My eyes followed the stones up the tall fireplace but stopped at the sight of three mounted heads. A deer, a boar, and…wait for it…a llama, stared back at me from the fireplace's stone wall. The llama's long neck stretched out over the hearth, its ears pointed forward. And in spite of the glassy stare in its eyes, it looked alert. Cake decorating or not, camp was creepy.

"I'm outta here," I said, turning around.

Dad blocked the doorway. "Oh no you're not."

"There's a llama head on the wall, Dad."

"So? Llamas are nice."

"Exactly my point. Who shoots a llama and then brags by hanging it on a wall?"

"Chloe, you're overreacting," said Mom, pulling me into the line for the check-in table. "Besides, you have to stay. How else will you learn how to decorate cupcakes for Mrs. Peghiny?"

She had a point. Not that it mattered. I had no choice but to stay.

Dad gave her a peck on her nose and she giggled. Oh no. I mean, don't get me wrong—I love that they love each other, but *really*? The only thing worse than PDA is *parents'* PDA. I looked around, cringing—had anyone else seen?

The line of people waiting to check in curved around the side of the fireplace and then disappeared. A couple feet ahead of us was a girl who looked my age. She gave an annoyed huff and shifted a unicorn Zoo 'n' You from her right arm to her left. She struggled to keep from poking her eyes out with the unicorn's horn while fighting with all the folds of the fabric. When she saw me staring at her, she stuck out her tongue. *How rude!*

Startled, I turned away from Rude Girl and came face-to-face with another girl.

Everything about her reminded me of a pogo stick—from the way she bounced on her toes in a never-ending rhythm to her curly hair. Based on how excited she looked, I'm pretty sure her skin struggled to keep her from exploding into millions of vibrating, springing particles.

Right then and there, I decided to call her Pogo.

Not to her face of course; that wouldn't be nice.

"Hey!" she said. "I'm Pauline but everyone calls me Paulie."

Or Pogo.

"I'm Chloe."

Dad elbowed me in the ribs. "See, you've made a friend already."

"Yeah, thanks, Dad."

"Wanna piece of gum?" Pogo held out a pack of gum.

I shrugged. "Sure. Thanks."

Dad turned to her. "Is this your first time to Camp Minnehaha?"

She nodded. "I'm uber-excited"—jump—"about the science"—jump—"I love tinkering around and inventing things"—bounce—"so when my dad heard about this camp, he signed me up"—double bounce—"plus, it gives

me a break from"—jump—"my little brothers and sisters"—
grand finale jump.

"Can you hold still for just a minute?" I asked. "I
can't focus."

She stopped and smiled.

Pogo stood twitching in place, which I guess was the
closest she could get to holding still. She put her hands in
her pockets and glanced at the back wall. "Whoa! Look at
the animals! Aren't they cool? My uncle once had a guinea
pig named Captain Nemo that he totally loved. When it
died, he put it in the freezer until he could have it mounted.
He even had the taxidermy guy make a small submarine to
keep it in." She frowned. "Whenever we visit, I see it staring
out a porthole."

Dad chuckled. "Your uncle must really enjoy reading
Twenty Thousand Leagues Under the Sea to have Nemo pre-
served in a submarine."

"Yeah, well, he draws pictures for kids' books and says he
likes to have Nemo around for 'inspiration.'" She put up finger quotes when she said *inspiration*. "Pretty radical, I know."

"I'll say," Mom muttered. She probably thought the
uncle needed a few therapy sessions.

Inspiration? In my experience, animals caused confu-
sion, not inspiration. I thought back to the day when my

hamster, What, escaped. The conversation I had with my parents about his disappearance is still stuck in my head.

Me: "Have you seen What?"

Dad: "Who?"

Me: "Not who. What."

Mom: "What?"

Me: "Yes."

Dad: "Huh?"

Me: "Never mind."

After checking in, and armed with cabin assignments, my parents and I headed back out to say good-bye. I gave them a hug and kiss and watched them climb in the van. Driving down the dirt road toward the exit, they put down the windows and waved a final time. I smiled and raised my hand in return, but when I looked closer, I saw they were actually waving their cruise tickets in the air. I'm pretty sure I heard cheering too. I blinked back tears, turned, and stared off in the direction of the cabins. I hoped I'd fare better than the llama.

Sunday, June 13
Get Run over by a Goat

. . . .

"Aww, man!" Pogo grumped. "I can't believe we have coun-
selors sleeping in our cabin. It's a total bummer. Now we
can't sneak around at night and do stuff."

"Like what?" I said, hauling my suitcase up the front
porch steps to our cabin. "I mean, seriously, what would we
have done anyway?"

"I don't know, but now we'll never find out, will we?"
She winked.

Pogo had just about vaulted herself through the roof
of the *Reg st ation Off ce* when she learned we'd both been
assigned to the Dakota cabin. But you know, maybe I almost did too, because it *was* nice to already know one of
my cabin mates.

Minutes later, we stood in the doorway of Dakota. Six
bunk beds lined the walls of the room, leaving the center of
the floor clear for what I assumed would be cabin meetings
or some such thing. I did the math and couldn't see how

twelve girls could possibly fit into such a small space. No matter where we all slept, we'd be packed in like sardines.

No one else was there, but some beds already had sleeping bags and junk on them. A couple bunks had Zoo 'n' Yous—one was a polar bear and the other a giraffe. The mattresses ranged in thickness from pizza box to shoebox. Stained indoor-outdoor gray carpeting was peeling up in the corners and a section near the front door looked like something had eaten it.

One bunk, with a shoebox-type mattress, had color-coordinated luggage—three suitcases plus a makeup tote, all with the same paisley pattern. I like luggage as much as the next girl, but this was a bit much. The word *diva* was embroidered in gold thread across the top of the sleeping bag, which also matched the luggage. I raised a brow at a familiar Zoo 'n' You unicorn on the bunk.

Looking around the room, I pointed to a bunk in the corner. "Those mattresses seem pretty good. How 'bout them?"

"Works for me."

"Do you want the top or the bottom?" I asked.

"Top, if that's okay with you."

"Go for it," I said, plunking my suitcase onto the mattress.

A humongous pink-tiled bathroom was attached to our cabin. Even though the place was air-conditioned and appeared civilized, I did a quick spider check. The last thing I needed was some creepy-crawly joining me in the shower.

And there it was.

In the far right corner of the ceiling.

Maybe a brown recluse. Possibly a black widow. Even if it was only a wimpy daddy longlegs, I wanted it dead. I briefly entertained the idea of showering with Bug-Me-Not instead of shampoo, but decided if it got in my eyes, I'd blind myself for life. As much as I hated spiders, I didn't want to go blind. Spraying the spider was the better idea.

I dashed back to my bunk, opened my luggage, and grabbed my bug spray.

Pogo looked up from her suitcase, puzzled. "What-cha doing?"

"Taking care of an eight-legged problem in the bathroom."

She nodded and continued to unpack her things.

I tried to think of the best tactical approach to spraying the spider. I wasn't sure how far the bug spray would reach—I hoped all the way to the corner—but a little extra height wouldn't hurt. I went into the toilet stall closest to the spider and stood on the seat. I stretched my arm as high as it would reach and unleashed rapid-fire squirts of Bug-Me-Not onto the web. The spider scrambled around and fell. I screamed and jerked away from the wall, forgetting where I stood. My right foot slipped into the toilet and my shoe filled with water.

Supergross.

Pogo popped her head in the bathroom. "Hey, we're supposed to be in the mess hall at three. It's time for us to go."

I yanked my wet foot out of the toilet and followed Pogo out the bathroom.

"I need to change shoes first."

She cocked her head.

"Don't ask." I pulled on fresh socks and then quickly slipped into dry shoes, not bothering to double-knot the laces.

Pogo whacked at the bushes and ferns with a large stick as she boinged along a dirt path. The whole world was her personal trampoline. I kicked at pinecones and noticed my left shoe was coming untied. "Do we even know how to get to the mess hall?" I said.

"Naaa."

I laughed at Pogo. "Nice goat imitation."

"Huh?"

"You said 'naaaa.' Just like some goat."

"No, I didn't," she said.

"Yes, you did."

She stopped. Her face turned slightly red. "I didn't say *anything*!"

I slapped at a mosquito on my neck and bent over to tie my shoe. "I thought I heard—"

"Look out!" Pogo yelled.

Something rammed into my rear end.

I launched into the air. My arms windmilled wildly, and I landed facedown in the dirt.

"Ugh." I rolled over to see who had kicked me from behind and…came face-to-face with a goat.

With bad breath.

Really bad breath.

I yelped and scooted backward until I was up against a pine tree.

The goat lowered its head and scuffed at the ground like it was going to charge. I scrambled up a couple of low-lying branches.

Instead of charging, the goat trotted over and chomped on the grass at the base of the tree.

I scowled and jumped down. My hands were sticky with sap and my hair was full of pine needles. I'm sure my head looked like a pincushion.

"Oh my word! That was the craziest thing ever!" Pogo said. "You okay?"

"Naaa."

I turned to the goat. "She wasn't asking you, moron."

The goat shook his head and then leaped over a rotted tree trunk and disappeared through some bushes.

I patted myself down, searching for blood or bones sticking out.

"Stupid goat." I dusted myself off. "Someone ought to put *that* animal on a wall. What kind of place allows a goat to run around and ram campers in the rear end?"

Pogo busted out laughing.

I didn't find it quite so funny. At least Pogo was the only one who saw. "Let's just get to the mess hall before a herd of cattle stampedes through here."

Rounding the path, we came to another gigantic log cabin. A wooden porch wrapped around the sides. Several campers sat in rocking chairs. Others sat on benches scattered around or leaned against the porch railing. I half expected a sign out front to read *Country Store*, instead of *Mess Hall*. Surprisingly, *this* sign had all its letters.

The mess hall sat at the top of a steep hill.

"C'mon, let's check out the view from the railing," I said.

A few feet from where we stood at the railing, the ground took a sharp dive, eventually leveling off near a building far below.

"Holy cow! Look how crazy that drop is!" Pogo said, leaning over the rail.

I joined her. "Man! Imagine sledding down *that* during the winter."

"We call *that* Mess Hall Hill—there's a ravine on the other side you need to stay away from."

I turned.

Director Mudwimple grasped a glass of iced tea in her chubby fingers. Tiny beads of perspiration dotted her forehead, prompting wisps of gray hair to coil. With the curls framing her face, she looked like Mrs. Claus more than ever. She took one look at me, and her free hand flew to her chest, while her other hand—the one holding the iced tea—sloshed its contents onto the wooden planks of the porch.

"Good gracious, dear! You look like you lost a barn brawl!" She pulled a twig and a couple of pine needles out of my hair.

Pogo snorted.

I dodged away from the iced tea that was swinging toward me. "Uh, about that. We were walking along a trail and—"

"Oh, that's wonderful, dear." She smiled wide. "We have many beautiful trails here. I hope you explore *all* of them and absorb the beauty of nature." She gestured widely and sloshed more of her tea onto the ground.

"But a goat—"

"Oh yes." Director Mudwimple nodded rapidly. "We have goats. We also have horses, cows, and chickens—all sorts of animals here at camp."

I gave up trying to tell her about the attack goat roaming the property. I sighed and gestured with my head. "So what's that building at the bottom?"

"That's the kitchen for the culinary arts—the cake decorating class," she said.

"There's a separate kitchen?"

"Sure is, sweetie." She waved her arm toward the mess hall as if showcasing a prize in a game show, spilling the rest of her drink. "This mess hall kitchen operates pretty much all day long. There's no room or time for y'all to be in here learning the fine art of frosting cakes! Do you know which elective you'll choose?" She stopped to take a sip of her tea and seemed surprised to find it empty. Then she turned her attention back to me. "When time comes to pick your elective, don't wait too long to make up your minds. There's a limited numbers of openings for each class. They fill up fast." She turned to talk to some kids next to us, not even waiting for our responses.

I shook my head. "Do you think it's the heat that makes her loony, or is she just like that?"

"Maybe she has ADHD," Pogo suggested.

"Can adults even have that?" I said.

"Sure, why not?"

"All campers inside for orientation!" a voice hollered.

The inside of the mess hall reminded me of our school cafeteria; just like at school, it was filled with several large, circular tables, except here, there was a large soda machine with free refills. That was a definite bonus in my book. I hoped the food would be tastier than school food. Or at least edible, which, let's face it, is not always the case with school food. Even though it was only three o'clock, delicious smells of garlic and butter already wafted through the air. I had high hopes.

"Find a table and take a seat," hollered the same voice.

The only tables with any seats left were in the back. At the center of each table stood a flagpole with a numbered flag.

"There's a table with empty seats back there." Pogo pointed. "Let's go before it fills up."

Table seven. I scowled.

Most people have lucky numbers. Not me. I have an *un*lucky number.

Seven.

On my seventh birthday I got the flu.

During the seventh inning stretch at my dad's annual

office softball game, I tumbled off the back of the bleachers and sprained my ankle.

On the Seven Twisters roller coaster, I sat—or rather, hung—upside down for an hour last summer when the ride malfunctioned.

I couldn't help but think this was a sign of bad things to come.

Sunday, June 13
Leave Pine Needles in Your Hair

. . . .

POGO YANKED MY ARM. "C'mon. There's a spot next to that kid with the soccer jersey."

She pointed.

A boy who seemed our age, wearing a Federación Ecuatoriana de Fútbol jersey, stood on a chair, staring into the crowd. He also looked familiar.

Standing next to him on the floor was a lanky, blond boy in a gray T-shirt with *MARINES* stamped across the front. I couldn't believe my luck.

"Sebastian! Nathan!" I yelled.

They turned toward us. I jumped up and down and waved madly. Nathan saw me before Sebastian did. He smiled and waved back—and my heart *might* have skipped a beat. Pogo yelped as I grabbed her arm and made for the back of the mess hall.

I pulled and squeezed Pogo through campers to unlucky table seven and to Nathan and Sebastian.

"Hey, guys."

Nathan pointed at my head. "You've got pine needles sticking out of your hair. What did you do? Roll in the bushes?"

I blushed and snatched at the needles the best I could. How embarrassing.

I turned to Nathan. "I can't believe you're both here! How crazy is that?"

"I know, right?" said Nathan.

Sebastian lightly punched Nathan in the shoulder. "I am here because Nathan's parents think he has no *amigos*." Sebastian was from Ecuador. He slipped in and out of Spanish more often than I daydreamed about Nathan.

I tilted my head to the side and looked at Nathan. "What's he talking about?"

Nathan laughed. "My folks are always nervous I'll have a hard time making friends since we move around so much. My dad heard about this place and thought it'd be fun. They said I could invite a friend." Nathan came from a military family and was new in town. Despite what his parents believed, he'd made lots of friends.

"Speaking of friends"—I turned to Pogo—"this is Pog—Paulie."

Sebastian turned to her and flashed a smile. "*Hola*."

"Hi." Pogo was bouncing on her toes again and didn't

seem to notice I'd stumbled over her name. "Y'all wanna piece of gum?"

Nathan had to time his hand to the same rhythm as she bounced in order take the moving stick of gum.

"I took Spanish last year," Pogo said. "Check this out, Sebastian: *Yo canto dulce como un sapo.*"

Sebastian raised his brow. "You sing sweet like a toad?"

"Oops." Pogo giggled. "That's not at all what I meant to say."

"So are you both in the same cabin?" Nathan asked.

"Yep—along with Diva," Pogo said.

"Who?" said Sebastian.

"Never mind," I said.

Nathan sat down and gestured to the chair next to him. He's cool like that. He doesn't mind being friends with a girl and doesn't act weird about sitting next to one—even one that has a teeny-tiny, secret crush on him. "So what do you think of camp so far?" he asked. His blond hair fell over his adorable eyes. He brushed it back.

"Well, let's see." I ticked the items off on my fingers. "There's a spider in the bathroom—or at least there was. I'm not really sure where it is now. Hopefully dead in a corner. Our camp director needs to switch to decaf, and a crazy goat attacked me. Oh…and we're here sitting at table number seven."

"Okay, you lost me at the goat and the number seven."

I opened my mouth to explain when Director Mudwimple clambered onto a small stage near the front of the mess hall. A humongous man sporting a baseball cap, armpit stains, and a whistle stood next to her. He looked like the Incredible Hulk—minus the weird green color and torn clothes. Director Mudwimple nodded to him and he blew his whistle, sending bits of spit cascading down on campers near him. Sitting near the back wasn't such a bad deal after all.

"Good afternoon, campers!" the director bellowed. "I have a couple quick announcements and then the instructors are going to introduce themselves. After that, we'll be off on a fun-filled tour of the campground. Sadly, I won't be joining you, as there's a minor issue involving one of our dear animals."

I was pretty sure the "minor issue" involved something with four legs, bad breath, and horns.

She sighed and took a deep breath. "Our goal at Camp Minnehaha is for everyone to have fun and be safe. In order for that to happen, we use a demerit system. If you choose not to follow our rules or show respect to others, you will be given a demerit. After five demerits, you're sent home."

Apparently, Mrs. Claus had a strict side to her. I had no worries about getting demerits—those were for troublemakers, not me.

She rattled on, hoped we'd all read all the rules in the welcome folders we were given at registration. Reminded us to pick our electives carefully. Encouraged us to enjoy the lovely trails but to always remember trail safety, blah, blah, blah. And then she was done. "Enjoy your tour. I leave you in good hands." She picked up a small halter and what looked like a leash and waddled away.

The Incredible Hulk spoke next. "My name's Coach Fox. I'm the sports instructor."

Duh.

A pretty lady with dark hair trapped under a hairnet and cheeks smudged with flour stepped onto the stage next. Coach Fox handed her a microphone. She smiled and put it to her mouth. "*Bonjour.* My name is Ms. Jacqueline. I am looking forward to working with each of you and introducing you to zee fine art of cake decorating." She paused. "Those who choose zis elective will prepare all zee desserts for a grand finale banquet for parents and campers on zee last day. It will be *fantastique!*"

"*Vive la France!*" someone yelled.

Ms. Jacqueline laughed and gave a wave with the mic before handing it off to the next instructor. Her laugh reminded me of twinkling lights—dainty and clear.

A man, who was wearing jeans, a pale-blue T-shirt, and

a stethoscope around his neck, helped Ms. Jacqueline down with one hand and took the mic with the other. Then he gave her a wink.

I nudged Pogo and whispered, "Did you see that? He just winked at her. *And* he held on to her hand a little too long for someone just taking a microphone. I bet he has a crush."

"He's too old to have a crush."

I rolled my eyes. "He's probably only forty."

"That's old," Pogo said. She looked to Sebastian.

"What?"

"Spanish is one of the romance languages," Pogo said. "What's your opinion?"

"I hate to tell you, but Spanish is a romance language because it comes from Latin. It has *nada* to do with love." He shook his head and looked down (but not before I saw him wink at Pogo).

The man onstage spoke. "I'm Dr. Mulholland. Y'all call me Doc."

"Or the Love Doctor," I whispered to Pogo.

She snorted and slapped her hand over her mouth.

"Now we have a crazy assortment of animals here at Minnehaha," Doc said with a southern drawl.

"He's right about the crazy part," I muttered.

Pogo giggled.

"And once y'all have met all the animals, I'm sure you'll feel quite at home around them. See y'all soon."

If he thought I'd ever feel at home with that goat (or spiders), *he* was the crazy one.

The science instructor, Mr. Dave, spoke last. Tall and tan, with a flowered shirt, jean cutoffs, and a ponytail, he looked like he should be surfing rather than doing experiments in a lab. "Yo! We do the same thing in the science lab that Ms. Jacqueline does in the kitchen—measurin' and mixin'. We just blow up our creations afterward!"

Cheers filled the cafeteria.

"Righteous!" Dave thrust a hang-loose sign in the air.

Pogo giggled. "He's kind of dreamy for a science guy."

Coach Fox rolled his eyes and jumped up next to Dreamy Dave. "Now that you've met everyone, we'll divide up into four teams. It's time for you campers to learn your way around! Tables one through three, follow me. Tables four through six, go with *May-dame-mo-sell* Jacqueline."

"I'm pretty sure he didn't say that right," I murmured.

Coach Fox continued. "Tables seven through nine, follow the good doctor. Ten through twelve, go with the mad scientist."

The noise of chairs scraping the floors and loud talking filled the room until everyone found the right team. We set off to explore the camp with Doc Mulholland leading the way.

Sunday, June 13
Visit the Funny Farm

. . . .

WE FOLLOWED DOC THROUGH a wooded trail and then climbed what the brochure mistakenly called a "gently rolling hill." It was clearly a mountain.

"Welcome to the farm!" Doc swept his arm toward the bottom of the hill.

My jaw dropped. I'd assumed there'd be a couple dogs, maybe a pony or two, the typical barn cat, and possibly a cow. One look at the view proved I'd completely underestimated Camp Minnehaha. An enormous, red barn with fenced-in yards at each stall stood in an open field. Wooden fences enclosed pastures where horses, cows, a few sheep, and, if I wasn't mistaken, a llama grazed. Running in and out of the enclosures were three sheep dogs. A cat sat on a wooden post, licking a front paw, while several chickens pecked at invisible objects in the dirt.

We made our way down the hill and stopped in front of the barn. I peeked around Pogo and counted twenty stalls—

some were empty; others weren't. Doc turned to face us, and we circled around to listen.

"Remember: this first week, y'all will get a chance to try all the electives. When you're here as veterinarians-in-training, there'll be lots to do. You'll learn the proper care of each animal, including feeding, cleaning, and even playing."

"What"—bounce—"do you mean"—bounce—"by playing?"—triple bounce—asked Pogo.

"Well, for one thing, each day, all ten of our horses will need to be exercised. One of the ways we do that is to take them out on the trails. We'll take turns, so each camper will get a chance to ride."

Pogo was practically shaking. I could tell it was taking all her self-control not to run over and jump on a horse and ride off into the sunset. I couldn't blame her though. The trail rides would definitely be the best part of being at the barnyard.

"I've shown horses for years," a voice behind me said.

I turned to see who spoke. It was Rude Girl.

She adjusted a bracelet on her wrist, and I saw a silver heart charm stamped with the word *diva*. I nudged Pogo in the ribs and pointed out the charm. It looked as though Rude Girl and our cabin diva were one and the same. Pogo rolled her eyes.

"Will we be riding English or Western?" Rude Diva

Girl batted her eyelashes at Doc. "I prefer English—it's more refined."

Doc smiled. "It's nice to know you have experience, young lady—"

"Victoria," she said. She combed her fingers through her already-perfect hair. She had the kind of hair that would have looked awesome on her show horse's tail. Long and straight and glossy enough to see a reflection in—I'm sure if Victoria knew she could see her own reflection in her hair, she'd stare at it all the time.

"Well, Victoria, to answer your question, we'll be riding Western. I've found over the years it's easier for those who are new to riding horses."

She pursed her lips and glowered at us. I got the feeling she wanted us to drop to our knees and beg her forgiveness since she wouldn't be as refined as she'd hoped.

Doc continued. "Now, during the second week, those of you who choose this as your elective will be assigned one animal that'll be yours to take care of for the entire week." He raised his hand for silence as a chorus of questions flew at him regarding who'd get the horses. "Everyone'll still get to ride them, even if you aren't assigned to one. Of course, I'll be here to help y'all with whatever you need. Any other questions?"

"How do we know which animal we'll get?" Nathan asked.

"We'll have a horseshoe tournament," said Doc.

"¿*Qué?*" Sebastian asked.

"I've got this," said Pogo. She faced Sebastian. "*Nos lavamos los cerdos con los zapatos.*"

Sebastian turned to Doc. "We will wash pigs with shoes?"

"Drat," Pogo said. "Really thought I had that one."

Doc chuckled. "Thankfully, no. You take an iron horseshoe and try to toss it onto a stake from about twenty feet away. The winner gets first pick of the animals, second place picks next, and so on."

"I think you might want a quick refresher course on your Spanish," I whispered to Pogo.

"No kidding," she said.

I could manage a basketball okay, but I'd never thrown a horseshoe before. I'd probably have better luck trying to slingshot a buffalo through a flaming Hula-Hoop. Good thing I wasn't planning on being at the barn the second week.

"Let's meet the animals," Doc said. He led the way through the giant barn door and stopped in front of a stall. "Our two goats are named King Arthur and Queen Guinevere."

His Royal Highness, King Arthur, was the same goat

that had head-butted me earlier (literally, his head to my butt). Now that I wasn't stuck in a tree, I got a better look at him. He was all white (kind of grimy, really) except for a black crown-shaped mark on his head between his two small horns. Probably the reason they called him King Arthur. He stood looking innocent in his stall, mindlessly chewing at a pile of loose hay. I narrowed my eyes and glared at him. He obviously thought nothing of his previous rough treatment of me. Actually, it would have surprised me if he had any thoughts at all. His pale, beady eyes were completely blank…like a ruthless predator.

"Now King Arthur suffers from a couple of things." Doc gave a gentle laugh. "The first being delusions of grandeur. He thinks he runs things around here, and he's a bit of a rascal. Most people don't know this, but goats are extremely intelligent animals and master escape artists. If he watches you work the lock a couple times, he'll practice and try to open it. The key is to lock the gate and check it twice—because if you leave it unlocked, His Highness will wander off." Doc patted the gate lock. "His second issue is that he faints."

I smacked a fly off my arm. "Wait. He does what?"

"He's a fainting, or myotonic, goat. These goats faint because of an inherited genetic disorder called myotonia. If they get frightened or overly excited, their muscles tense up and they fall over—sometimes with their legs sticking straight up in the air."

"Awesome," Nathan said.

"It only lasts for about ten seconds or so, and then they get up and keep going," Doc said.

The visual image of King Arthur lying flat on his back with all four knobby legs pointing toward the sky made me snort. It was almost as satisfying as the thought of his head mounted on a wall.

A wooden fort-looking thing stood in the center of King Arthur's paddock.

"What's that?" I asked, pointing to the structure.

Doc turned. "That's his climbing platform. Goats are excellent climbers and that's kind of like his playground."

Pogo nudged me in the ribs. "He really is adorable. Just look at those floppy ears!"

"Well, whoever gets to be his caretaker during the second week better keep him away from me."

We followed Doc through the barn, and every once in a while, he'd stop. If an animal was in its stall, he'd make introductions. Each animal's name hung on a plaque outside its sliding stall door, and all the stalls had a small, fenced-in yard attached to them.

I strolled past the names on the horse stalls.

Sunset.

Footloose.

Princess.

Road Rage.

Road Rage? I hoped I wouldn't get stuck with *that* horse for any trail rides. We came out the other end of the barn, and I scanned the pasture and tried to guess which horse was Road Rage. All twelve of them looked harmless—obviously, one of them was faking.

Sunday, June 13
9:32 p.m.

Guess what?!?! Nath♥n and Sebastian are here!
I was soooooo happy to see Nath♥n.

The instructors seem nice. Ms. Jacqueline (the
cake instructor) is French. She has a neat
accent—I guess Sebastian does too. If I had to
speak another language, I would be SO worried
about my accent—I doubt it would sound cool like
theirs do.

Director Mudwimple told us there's a ravine on the
other side of Mess Hall Hill that fills up crazy
fast with water when it rains—something about
a flash flood. No campers are allowed over there.
I guess she thinks we'll die...or something worse.

Every night during dessert, the instructors
choose one camper who has "demonstrated true
compassion" (those were Director Mudwimple's
exact words), and they give the person the
Distinction of Recognized Kindness award. Some

of the kids who've been here before say it's a big tradition and a HUGE deal to be picked.

A mean girl named Victoria is also in our cabin. She is SUPER picky about her stuff. A spider the size of a small island nation crawled up the wall near the bathroom door while I was brushing my teeth. (I'm pretty sure it was the same one I tried to kill earlier.)

The only thing in the bathroom to spray it with was hairspray—how was I supposed to know it was Victoria's "custom-made" hairspray? How can you custom make hairspray anyway?

I was like some half-crazed graffiti artist with that can. Victoria sure picked a bad time to open the bathroom door. After the nurse had her wash her eyes out for ten minutes, she was fine. I think she's making a PRIMA DONNA DIVA deal out of the fact I used up her whole can of hairspray on a spider—which, by the way, STILL didn't die. It crawled off to its secret lair somewhere— probably to admire its new hairdo.

Mindy, our counselor, was all "Spiders are an important and necessary part of our world—they kill bad bugs. Blah, blah, blah." She's never going to convince me spiders are necessary to my world!

A goat named King Arthur ran me over and then cornered me in a tree. Luckily, only Pogo saw. This place is bizarre.

Oh, and Doc Mulholland (the vet) has a crush on Ms. Jacqueline.

Good night.

Monday, June 14
Startle His Royal Highness

• • • • • • • • • • • • • • • •

DURING BREAKFAST ON MONDAY morning, Pogo and I looked at our schedule for the week. After eating, we were supposed to go back to our cabin for daily cleanup and to pick a cabin captain.

I pointed to the schedule. "What's a cabin captain?"

She shrugged. "I dunno. Someone who helps Counselor Mindy, I guess."

I didn't know much about my fellow bunk mates other than what I'd observed since arriving. Besides Mindy, there were eight of us in the Dakota cabin:

- Pauline (a.k.a. Paulie, a.k.a. Pogo),
  who should lay off the caffeine.
- Ruth, who, being homesick,
  blubbered before, during, and after
  dinner last night—and then cried
  herself to sleep.

- Charlotte, who's a bit of a busybody
  and told everyone about Ruth's
  homesickness.
- Marcie, whose snoring apparently
  blocked out the noise of Ruth's
  bedtime blubbering.
- Leslie, who cracks her knuckles
  more often than I take a breath.
- Victoria, whose need for lip gloss,
  air-conditioning, and hot water
  surpasses even Hollywood's most
  pampered stars.
- Anna, who quickly became Victoria's personal lackey.
- And me, the only normal kid.
  Thankfully, I don't have any issues.

Pogo and I finished our biscuits and gravy and carried our trays to the dish counter. Anna balanced Victoria's tray on top of her own while Victoria stood off to the side, rubbing strawberry-scented lotion on her arms.

"There's a good chance that's going to attract bugs, you know," Pogo said. "They like the stuff that smells nice."

"Doubt it," she sneered. "It's a custom-made bug repellent Daddy special ordered for me from Europe." She gave her left arm a final swipe. "It's *super*expensive."

I was all set for Pogo to haul off and give Victoria a snarky reply. Instead, she just smiled. "Isn't that nice." She linked her arm through mine. "C'mon, Chloe, let's head back to the cabin."

Victoria harrumphed and turned on her heel.

Outside and away from Victoria's diamond-studded ears, I turned to Pogo. "What was that all about?"

"My mom used to say a lady never tells somebody off, no matter how much of a Miss Priss they are. Instead, you just smile and say, 'Isn't that nice.' It's Southern-ese for 'go stick it in your ear.'"

Victoria's voice headed our way, and I tugged on Pogo's arm. "C'mon, let's take the other path to the cabin. I don't want to deal with her diva-ness yet."

We walked toward the back side of the mess hall, and as we rounded the corner, we stopped dead in our tracks.

King Arthur stood at the edge of Mess Hall Hill. No doubt he was surveying his kingdom. I grabbed Pogo and pulled her against the side of the building, out of sight of the dumb goat. I looked around for someone to tell he'd escaped from his pen, but I didn't see a soul. All the other campers had gone back to their cabins, and I assumed the instructors were at their stations, preparing for the day.

We were alone.

King Arthur was alone…standing with his back to me at the edge of a steep hill.

I looked at Pogo and put my finger to my lips. Nearby were several metal trash cans lined up next to a storage shed behind the mess hall. I tiptoed over and delicately lifted two lids. Holding one in each hand, I slinked over until I stood smack-dab behind King Arthur. I glanced over my shoulder one more time to make sure the coast was still clear. Then I crashed the lids together like a pair of cymbals.

King Arthur's legs shot out in all directions, and he fainted right then and there.

He immediately became a blur of black-and-white hair and hooves tumbling down Mess Hall Hill at ninety miles per hour.

"Oh no!" I squealed.

Pogo rushed over to where I stood. "I thought he'd just fall over—not break the sound barrier rolling down a hill."

"Me too! Do you think he's hurt? I didn't want to hurt him—just make him faint."

I held my breath, clutched the lids in my hands, and watched as the goat slid to a stop at the bottom. He struggled to his legs, shook his head, and took a couple wobbly steps.

Yay! I hadn't killed him! I breathed a sigh of relief. He looked back up the hill, and I quickly held up a lid in front of my face—not that he could even see that far, but still, now that the score was even, I didn't want him to know it was me. He trotted off (in an uneven line) in the direction of the barn.

Pogo tugged on my arm. "Oh my gosh, Chloe. That was crazy!"

"Tell me about it." I set the lids back on the trash cans. Scaring a goat down a hill wasn't very kind, but even I have my moments of weakness. I probably wouldn't be getting the Distinction of Recognized Kindness award anytime soon. "I'm glad he got up. At first I thought I had killed him."

Pogo snorted. "Chloe McCorkle, on the hillside, with trash can lids."

"Only this isn't a game of Clue. You can't tell anyone, okay?"

"My lips are sealed."

"Promise?"

"Sure."

I glanced down the hill once more to make sure King Arthur hadn't stumbled and died, and then we headed for our cabin to find out what in blazes a cabin captain was.

Monday, June 14
Put Victoria in Charge

. . . .

THE CABIN MEETING STARTED with all of us sitting in a circle on the floor. Actually, Victoria wore her Zoo 'n' You and sat on Anna's folded blanket. Everyone else sat on the stained carpet. Mindy sat between Victoria and Ruth and would occasionally pat Ruth's back and hand her a tissue.

"Okay!" Mindy chirped. "Let's get to know each other a little more before we head off to our first elective of the day." She looked at each one of us and smiled. Her teeth were absolutely perfect—the kind that dentists use for billboard advertisements. "This is my third year as a counselor, but Director Mudwimple is my aunt, so I've basically spent all my summers here. I'm the head counselor this time, so in a little bit, I'll need to head out to meet briefly with the other cabins."

Director Mudwimple was her aunt? That explained the perkiness—must be a family trait.

"If you have any questions or get homesick or anything,"

continued Mindy, "just let me know. I've seen it all and I'm here to help." She handed Ruth another tissue.

I raised my hand. "How come our cabin sleeps twelve, but there's only nine of us?"

She winked. "That's a perk of being the director's niece—we can spread out a bit more and have some privacy."

In a cabin this small, I could look for privacy all day and never find it.

"Let's start with a fun, getting-to-know-you game. Everyone say their first and last name, and then share one thing special about yourself that begins with the same letter as your last name!"

"Only one?" Victoria said, pushing out her lower lip into a pout.

Mindy giggled. "I'll go first. I'm Mindy Carmelo, and I'm *captain* of the cheer squad at Sponsler University." She emphasized *Carmelo* and *captain*, as though we needed the reminder they both began with the same letter. She flashed another dentist-advertising smile, put her left hand on her hip, and thrust her right fist into the air. "Goooooooo Tarantulas!"

My jaw dropped. "You're kidding, right? Your mascot is a spider?"

She clapped. "Totally cool, isn't it?"

"So, during football games, there's some guy running around the field in an eight-legged costume, getting the crowd all excited?"

"Yep, but it's not a mean-looking spider. It's wearing a football helmet and pads."

"Oh." At least the spider practiced safety first. How comforting.

Mindy turned to Ruth. "Would you like to go next?"

She sniffed and shook her head.

"That's okay. We'll come back to you." She leaned over to me. "How about you, sweetie?"

"My name's Chloe McCorkle, and my special thing is *maybe* I can take the cake decorating elective so I can earn money for a bike I want." I also hoped that *maybe* she'd accept that as my special fact. I wasn't good at coming up with interesting things about myself, and I've never liked being put on the spot.

"If you can get into that elective, I'm sure you'll have a wonderful time in the kitchen. That class is superpopular and usually fills up first."

Not cool. I'd need to come up with a plan to make sure I'd make it into that elective.

Mindy looked past me to Marcie. "How about you?"

"I'm Marcie Asher, and I'm *allergic* to horses. I'm really

sorry if I snore at night. I'm taking allergy medicine, but I don't know if it's working."

Victoria looked up from filing her nails. "It's not."

Marcie smiled weakly. "Sorry."

Pogo shrugged. "It's not your fault. My cat snores back home, and it's really loud. You're not as bad as my cat."

"Thanks." Marcie looked confused. "I think."

Eventually, we made it around to Victoria. She let her Zoo 'n' You fall dramatically from her shoulders and repositioned herself on her blanket. She brought her hair around to the front and let it fall over her left shoulder. "My name is Victoria and something special—"

"Wait!" Mindy said. "What's your last name?"

Victoria sighed. "Radamoskovich."

Mindy cocked her head. "Radamoskovich? That's a very unique name. Are you related to the football player who won the Heisman trophy this past year—JT Radamoskovich?"

Victoria rolled her eyes. "Yes, and my special fact beginning with *R* is I'm *really* sick of hearing about my brother." She leaned in. "All. The. Time."

I wasn't a huge sports person, but even I had heard of JT Radamoskovich. During college football season, Dad and I would curl up on the sofa and watch games together while Mom hit garage sales. Sportscasters drooled over the straight-A, all-American quarterback. He was just drafted to play for the Dallas Cowboys. He was the perfect kid.

Mindy blinked repeatedly at Victoria. "Well…I can see how…someone as talented as your brother could cast a big shadow."

Victoria narrowed her eyes.

"How about," Mindy said, "you share another special fact—about you this time?"

Victoria looked at me. "I plan on taking the cake decorating elective as well—I think it will be fun to have a cake competition with our chef when I get home. Oh, and another thing special about me is I won the Miss Somerset Beauty Pageant last month."

Leave it to her to sneak in one more fact about herself. Sheesh.

Mindy blinded us with another smile. "How marvelous! Well, I for one am so excited to get to know all of you more. If you need anything, just ask me." She picked up a clipboard that was in front of her.

"The next thing we need to do is pick a cabin captain. The cabin captain is the person who will make sure everything is tidy and ready for inspection each day. Cabins are awarded points based on how clean they are. The one with the most points at the end of our two weeks earns a prize."

Victoria's hand shot up. "I think I should be cabin captain. After all, I have lots of experience at camps, so I know what to do."

Mindy nodded. "That's true—experience might be very helpful. This is something we vote on though. Does anyone want to second the nomination?"

Victoria elbowed Anna, who immediately raised her hand.

"I do," Anna said.

"Perfect!" Mindy said.

Pogo nudged me and whispered, "You be cabin captain. You don't want Victoria in charge."

"No way. She already hates my guts for using all her hairspray on the spider." I knew if I went up against her and won, she'd make my life at camp miserable. But then, the idea of Victoria being queen of the cabin was enough to make me risk it.

I turned to Mindy. "I'd like to be cabin captain too."

"Okay. Does anyone second Chloe's nomination?"

Pogo raised her hand. "She's got my vote."

Victoria glared in our direction.

Mindy stood. "All right. We'll put it to the vote. I'll give everyone a piece of paper, and you write the name of the person you want. Then, I'll tally the votes and we'll see who wins."

"Anyone who votes for me can use my nail polish—it's from Italy."

Mindy giggled. "Victoria, you can't bribe the voters, silly."

Mindy tore eight sheets of paper from her notebook and handed them out. "Spread out so you have privacy, and vote. Then give them to me when you're done."

Pogo scribbled down her vote and handed her folded paper back to Mindy before I had even finished writing my name. Anna took one look at Victoria's nails and wrote her choice. Charlotte paused for a moment and then cast her vote. Marcie, Ruth, and Leslie hunched over their papers and scribbled names down. Mindy tallied the results.

Victoria: 6.

Me: 2.

Apparently, you *can* bribe voters.

Monday, June 14
Delight in Flushing Toilets

. . . .

MINDY TOSSED THE BALLOTS into the trash can and pulled a paper from her clipboard. "Here's the list of things that need to be done each day before inspection. I have to go to the counselor meeting now, but since Victoria's an experienced camper, I know I'm leaving you in great hands. I'll be back before we have to leave for our first elective. Ta-ta!" She smiled a megawatt smile and then was gone.

We stared at Victoria as she looked over the list. "I think the best thing to do is to assign everyone a chore."

That actually sounded fair—I was surprised. Maybe it wouldn't be too bad with her in charge. She glanced around the cabin and then down at the list in her hand one more time.

"First, everyone needs to make their beds. While you all do that, I'll write names next to chores." She turned to Anna. "Will you pretty please make my bed while I work on this chore chart?"

She nodded.

"Sorry you didn't win," Pogo said to me as she climbed the ladder to her top bunk.

"Yeah, me too. Thanks for voting for me though."

I tidied my sleeping bag and fluffed up my pillow. Since it was only the first real day at camp, my luggage was still nice and orderly. I didn't have to do much with my clothes.

Pogo landed on the floor with a thud from the top bunk. "Where's Victoria?"

I turned around. "I don't know. She was here a minute ago."

Anna walked up. "Victoria finished the list and went to take a shower."

"Oh?" Pogo said. "Did she work up a sweat with all the writing?"

"Huh?"

"Never mind," Pogo said. "Where's the list?"

Anna pointed to the wall near the bathroom door.

"Good grief," I muttered.

Victoria had posted the chore list to the wall using tape covered with unicorns and hearts.

— Empty trash can: Anna
— Vacuum floor: Marcie

- Clean mirrors: Charlotte
- Pick up outside trash: Ruth
- Sweep front porch: Leslie
- Scrub toilets: Paulie and Chloe

"I say we impeach her," I said.

"I bet this is just for today. We'll probably have a different chore tomorrow," Pogo said.

"We'd better—'cause I'm not cleaning bathrooms for two weeks." I looked at the list again. "Where's *her* name on this anyway?"

Anna looked uncertain. "She said *her* job is to make sure everyone else does their job."

I stared at her, grinding my teeth together. "Isn't… that…nice."

Pogo pulled me toward the bathroom door. "C'mon. We can't leave for the elective until we get this done."

Billows of steam assaulted us when we walked through the bathroom door. "How are we even supposed to *find* the toilets in here?" I said, waving my hand through the air.

"Here." Pogo handed me a toilet brush. "You take the two stalls near the showers, and I'll take the two near the wall."

I started to walk toward the bathroom stalls, but Pogo pulled me back.

"Hold on a minute." She bounced on her toes and whispered, "Do you know what happens when a toilet is flushed while the shower is on?"

"No."

Pogo gave me a mischievous grin. "Well, having younger brothers and sisters in the house who don't *care* if someone is in the shower, I've learned it takes a while before the hot water returns."

We slapped high fives and went to our separate stalls.

I went to the first stall, swirled the brush around the bowl, and was filled with a huge sense of pleasure when I flushed the toilet and Victoria yelped from the unexpected surge of cold water. Pogo leaned out her stall door, winked, and flushed her own toilet a couple of times.

"You two better quit that or I'm going to tell," Victoria screeched.

"What are you going to say? That we were cleaning the toilets and just making sure they were scrubbed good? Yeah, that'll get us in trouble for sure," Pogo said. She made a face, mocked Victoria silently…and flushed one more time.

Victoria muttered and I snickered while making my way to the next toilet stall.

Before I even had the stall door open all the way, I saw the spider. How it survived the Bug-Me-Not dousing, the fall from the corner, and the hairspray soaking was beyond me. I wasn't about to let it get away a third time though.

I gripped my toilet brush in front of me and slowly advanced. I'd never killed a spider with a toilet brush before. I'd used shoes, a book, even a hair dryer. But never a toilet brush. I wasn't sure it could be done.

I jabbed at it, and it scurried up the wall several feet. I jabbed once more, and it darted closer to the shower stall on my left. I had one shot left before it disappeared into the rising steam of Victoria's shower. This spider was going to wish he was the one wearing football pads and a helmet. I balanced myself on the toilet seat (again) for a final blow. I raised the brush over my head and *smack!*

The spider fell into the shower stall.

Victoria screamed.

And I fell into the toilet…again.

Monday, June 14
Open Personal Mail in a Public Area

• • • • • • • • • • • • • • • •

BEFORE LUNCH MONDAY, DIRECTOR Mudwimple called me to her office.

She motioned for me to sit when I came in. "Miss McCorkle, we seem to have a problem." She picked up a pink paper and turned it around for me to read. The words *Disciplinary Action Report* were typed bold-faced across the top. "A kitchen aide reported seeing you clang trash can lids together, scaring poor King Arthur half out of his wits this morning." She pushed her glasses to the top of her head and scowled. "What do you have to say in regards to that?"

I swallowed and cleared my throat. "In my defense, he was clearly more than half out of his wits already. I probably just scared what was left."

She stared at me. "You're not helping your case, young lady. We take our responsibility for the animals very seriously, and showing cruelty to them is something I *will not* tolerate at Camp Minnehaha."

"Yes, ma'am—I'm sorry. I wasn't trying to be cruel."

"You have one demerit. Try not to get any more." She stood and reached for her glasses on her head. "You're dismissed for lunch."

I ate lunch and acted as though I wasn't the kid who got the first demerit at camp. Demerits weren't for people like me—I was a good kid. If word got out, everyone would think I was a troublemaker. My lips were sealed—I wasn't about to even tell Pogo. Plus, Director Mudwimple didn't seem to know Pogo was there. It was entirely that stupid goat's fault—he'd better not show his face to me again or trash can lids would be the least of his problems.

During dessert, Director Mudwimple stood on the stage to holler out announcements. Free time until 2:00 p.m. Cherokee won cleanest cabin award. Whoever took the *M* off the welcome sign needed to return it—enough letters were already missing, thank you very much. Then, Director Mudwimple called me forward to pick up a shoebox-sized care package from Mom and Dad.

I grabbed my box and scurried back to the table where Pogo, Sebastian, and Nathan sat.

"How did you get a care package already?" Pogo asked. "It's only the first day of camp."

"I don't know." I tore off the brown paper and let the

shreds fall to my feet. "Mom must have overnighted it." She was the best.

I took the lid off to see what treasures the box held.

Nathan snorted.

Sebastian leaned in for a closer look. "*¿Que es eso?*"

Mr. Snuffles stared up at me with his mismatched eyes—I swear, he was grinning.

Nooooooo!

I snatched the note that lay on top and fumbled to replace the lid as fast as possible before anyone else could see.

Dear Chloe,

We hope you're having a fun time at camp. We miss you already. Here are some M&M's and Skittles. I also have enclosed $10 for you to spend at the camp store—don't spend it all on soda! I thought you might need some more sunscreen, so I added that, plus a photo of you, Dad, and me.

Love,

Mom

PS When we got back from dropping you off, I noticed you forgot to pack Mr. Snuffles. I know you sleep with him every night, and I'm sure you're missing him. I'm so glad I found him under the pillow in your room. Surprise! Here he is!

Victoria walked up from behind Nathan. "Well, well, look who got a care package from Mommy and Daddy."

With a swift flick of a finger, she popped the lid off and peered into the box.

"OMG," she squealed, yanking Mr. Snuffles out of the box and holding him up for all the mess hall to see. "It's so nasty!" She laughed and waved him around. Snickers and giggling filled the air around me.

"Give it back, Victoria." I snatched him away and shoved him in the box, then slammed the lid down.

Victoria draped her arm around my shoulder. "You know, baby Chloe, if you want a nice stuffed animal that doesn't smell, you can borrow my Zoo 'n' You. All you need to do is ask."

More kids laughed. Thankfully, Pogo wasn't one of them.

I pushed Victoria's arm off me. "And take away your only friend?"

Pogo laughed this time.

"Ouch," Nathan said.

Victoria's eyes narrowed. She turned on her heel and walked away.

Heat raced up my neck. I wanted to crawl under a table and stay there. I shoved Mom and Dad's card inside the box and snatched up the trash on the floor.

"I'm headed back to the cabin," I said.

Pogo bounded up to the trash cans with me. "I'll come with you—you cool with that?"

I nodded but stayed quiet until we reached our cabin.

I tossed the box on the bed and Mr. Snuffles bounced out as it dumped over. "I left him home on purpose," I said through clenched teeth.

"Why?" Pogo picked him up.

"Because of people like Victoria."

"He's cute—and you've obviously had him for a long time."

I hung my head. "I didn't want anyone making fun of me or thinking I was a baby."

"Victoria has her dumb Zoo 'n' You—and so do Anna and Marcie. No one thinks they're babies."

"That's different. Zoo 'n' Yous are really popular. It's okay to have them."

Pogo looked sympathetic. "I get it. I wanted to bring my favorite blanket, but my dad wouldn't let me. He said it might get lost or something." She held Mr. Snuffles out to me.

I took him and looked at his worn-out condition. "Yeah. My grandpa gave Mr. Snuffles to me when I was little. Mr. Snuffles reminds me of him." I hugged the stuffed animal. "Grandpa died a couple years ago."

"My mom died when I was seven, so I totally get what you mean. Dad gave me her jewelry box and it's my favorite thing in the whole world."

"Your mom died?" I'd never met anyone who had a parent who had died. I wasn't sure what to say. "I'm sorry."

"It's okay." She shrugged. "Things were really hard at first, and they still are at times, but I do the best I can with it. It can be a bummer when there's stuff at school like mother-daughter events, but my dad comes to those." She gave a small laugh. "Last year, my school had a Mother's Day tea and everyone was with their moms, and there was my dad, sipping tea and eating a scone with me."

"Were you embarrassed?"

"I stopped caring what people thought about my dad a long time ago." She was silent for a moment. "Dad once told me there are two types of opinions in the world—the ones that matter, and the ones that don't. And if I spend my time worrying about the stuff that isn't important, then I'll miss seeing what really is."

I traced around Mr. Snuffles's mismatched eyes with my finger. "I don't mind standing out from a crowd if it's for a good reason—something totally crazy like if I saved someone's life or something, but generally speaking, I'd rather blend in. I'm not saying I'll jump off a cliff if everyone else does, but I just prefer to play it safe." I unzipped my sleeping bag and shoved Mr. Snuffles to the bottom. "I'll bring him out at night."

Pogo shrugged. "It's your call, but I wouldn't feel ashamed of someone or something you love just because of Victoria." She glanced at Victoria's bunk. "Personally, I think she has issues."

I knew Victoria's type. People like her had the power to make my life miserable—whether I was at camp or in middle school. I might as well paint a target on my back that said *Dork—publicly humiliate me.* The best thing to do was lay low and not draw attention to myself.

Easier said than done.

Monday, June 14
8:56 p.m.

WORST DAY EVER!!!

Victoria made Pogo and me clean the bathroom, since we didn't want her to be cabin captain (she was voted captain anyway ☹). That's how a spider ended up on Victoria. How was I supposed to know it was going to fall on her head while she was in the shower? Guess I just got lucky.

Mom thought I left Mr. Snuffles at home on accident—which I DID NOT—and she mailed him to me! Victoria waved him all around the mess hall, and now a bunch of Victoria wannabes are calling me a baby.

Pogo says not to worry about Victoria, but I DON'T want people to think I'm a dumb little baby. I gave Pogo the Skittles that were in my care package—a way to say thanks for being my friend and NOT making me feel stupid.

I found out today that Pogo's mom died when she was seven. I don't know what I would do if my mom or dad ever died. Pogo said she and her dad build all kinds of stuff in their garage—weird, right?!?!

Today at lunch, we were talking about all the electives. Pogo really wants to do science, but I pointed out that hardly any other girls are doing that one. She just shrugged and said that was fine. Not me! She doesn't seem to get bothered by things like that or people like Victoria—I guess that's what happens when you lose a parent. You just stop caring about what others think about you.

I got revenge on King Arthur for ramming me into the dirt yesterday. I made him faint, and he somersaulted down Mess Hall Hill—which is practically the Grand Canyon. I'm glad he's okay though. At least he didn't roll down the part that turns into the ravine. ROGL (Rolling On the Grass Laughing). Pogo and I swore each other to secrecy but Director Mudwimple found out about it anyway—now I have a demerit!!! I WON'T be getting more, that's for sure!

I saw Doc Mulholland holding Ms. Jacqueline's hand during free time! They were taking a walk. I told Pogo about it, but she still isn't convinced he has a crush on her. I don't know what it would take to convince her—a wedding?!

Oh, and some girl named Rory got the Distinction of Recognized Kindness for helping one of her friends learn how to swim. I guess that's pretty nice.

Wednesday, June 16
Throw a Chicken

. . . .

VICTORIA THOUGHT IT WAS great fun to do elephant imper-
sonations with her arms whenever she saw me. She must have
figured out I kept Mr. Snuffles hidden in my sleeping bag
because during cabin cleanup, she made a big deal about acci-
dentally throwing him away because she thought he was a
rag. Good thing Pogo was there to hold me back from taking
Victoria's custom shower gel and squirting it all over her face.

I decided the best way to keep Mr. Snuffles safe was
to keep him with me. I emptied my messenger bag of my
toiletries and hairbrush and stuffed Mr. Snuffles and a water
bottle inside. I slung it across my body, and we headed to
our first elective of the day—sports.

As we approached the playing fields, Coach Fox
glanced at his watch. I guess we were late because Nathan
and Sebastian's cabin was already throwing Frisbees back
and forth on what looked like a football field, just a tad
smaller. I dropped my satchel near the bleachers.

"Line up for roll call," hollered Coach Fox. "Dakota cabin stand here and Kalaqua there. When I call your name, grab either a red or yellow jersey, and jog to center field." He grabbed his clipboard. At least it wasn't going to be boys against girls. Maybe I would even get on the same team as Nathan.

"Carl Jamison, red team. Marcie Asher, yellow team. Nathan Maddux." He looked up. "How 'bout I call you Mad Dog?"

"That's cool," Nathan said. "Which team?"

"Red." He checked his clipboard again. "Leslie Santamaria, yellow. Victoria Radamoskovich—" Coach Fox stopped. "Radamoskovich?"

Victoria exhaled loudly. "Yes?"

"Any relation to JT Radamoskovich?"

She looked like she wanted to say no.

"He's her brother," Charlotte offered.

Victoria growled.

"Cool," some kid from the Kalaqua cabin said. "Could you get me his autograph?"

Victoria whirled around, teeth bared, and was about to launch an attack on the poor kid when Coach Fox sidled up next to her, seemingly oblivious to the fact she wanted nothing more than to maul a fellow camper.

"Well, isn't that something?" Coach Fox said. "He's got

the best arm I've seen on a quarterback in a long time. Your team will be lucky to have you today—you're on red."

Victoria gave him a smile that I'm sure translated to *I hope you choke on your whistle.* She yanked a jersey over her head and stomped out to center field.

Nathan and I ended up on different teams—major bummer. At least Pogo and I were on the same team.

The game Coach Fox had picked for us was Ultimate Frisbee. I'd never played before, but Coach Fox said it was basically football with a Frisbee, minus the tackling, and once you held the Frisbee, you couldn't move, except to throw it to a teammate.

By halftime, Nathan's team was beating ours six to three, but it was a seriously fun game. I grabbed my water bottle and joined Pogo on the bleachers.

Victoria sashayed by, talking to Anna. "Let's go sit in the shade. I don't want to end up looking like frizzy-haired, red-faced Chloe."

I reached back and touched my hair. All the running around had loosened my ponytail. Curls sprogged in every direction. I wondered if Nathan noticed my frizzy hair and red face. I ran my fingers through the tangled mess. It was a lost cause. Time for a new strategy: don't run so fast. At least that might keep my face from looking like a big, fat tomato.

I spent most of the second half listening to Coach Fox holler at me to hustle and get moving. I'm pretty sure the only reason he wasn't hollering the same thing at Victoria was because of her brother. We didn't score any points during the second half, and Nathan's team creamed us 10–3.

I picked up my satchel, made sure Mr. Snuffles was safe, and then checked my schedule.

"Where y'all fixing to go next?" Nathan said, walking up to me.

"The barn."

Standing a few feet behind him, Victoria brushed out her long hair. She didn't have a drop of sweat on her. Not fair.

"Have fun," he said. "We'll catch y'all at lunch, right?"

"Yeah. Good game, by the way," I said.

Victoria bent forward and then flipped her head back, her hair followed in a gorgeous arc and landed smoothly down her back.

Nathan nodded. "Back at ya. What was up with you slowing down the second half?" he said.

"Guess I got tired," I said.

I dropped the satchel and tried the same move as Victoria, bending over and throwing my head back.

"Are you okay?" Nathan asked.

My hair was about as opposite as you could get from

Victoria's. I probably looked pretty ridiculous, and I think I pinched a nerve in my neck.

"Yeah—I thought there was a bee. That's all." I grabbed my satchel and walked away before I did anything else stupid. *Note to self—next time, skip the neck injury and simply write MORON across your forehead—it's faster, less painful, and just as effective.*

"See ya at lunch," I called over my shoulder.

Doc Mulholland said we were going to take the horses out on a trail ride. Pogo squealed. I still wasn't sure which horse was Road Rage, but luckily, Doc picked out Sunset for me. She was a beautiful, chestnut-red color, and he reassured me she was "sweet as a Pixy Stick." I searched out the perfect place to hide my satchel. Three large, wooden barrels were stacked on top of each other near Sunset's stall. The top barrel was probably close to fifteen feet in the air.

Perfect.

Hay bales against the wall created a somewhat squishy, unstable staircase, but I made it to the top. I tossed the satchel onto the top barrel and climbed down, almost landing on Victoria.

"Watch what you're doing!" she barked. She looked at the hay bales and barrels. "What were you doing up there?"

I shrugged. "Nothing."

"Fine. Don't tell me. It's not like I care about you or anything you do." She shrugged and walked away.

I waited until she went around the corner by the tack room and then headed outside to find Sunset.

Doc stood holding the reins of a dark brown horse. "This handsome guy is Chester. For those of you who've never ridden before, Chester and I are going to show you how to get into the saddle." He moved to the left side of his horse and transferred the reins to his left hand. "While still holding on to the reins, put your left foot into the stirrup, grab the saddle, and swing up and into the seat."

I'd never mounted a horse before and figured I was in for trouble. I was right. Despite the fact that Sunset stood perfectly still, it would've been easier to climb on top of a rampaging gorilla. It was a struggle getting my left foot into the stirrup, let alone getting my body to face the right direction in the saddle.

Ten minutes later, we were all lined up and Doc did a final stirrup check to make sure they were at the right length for everyone. One horse, Daisy, stood patiently without her rider.

"Where's Victoria?" Doc said, looking around.

Victoria sauntered over from the barn. "Sorry, Doc," she said. "I had to visit the bathroom first."

"Mount up and we'll get started."

Victoria was so graceful, she practically floated up to the saddle. She turned her head my way and smiled slyly. Show-off.

It was taking all of my concentration to stay upright on Sunset—and we hadn't even started the ride. I didn't have the energy to put up with her high horse attitude.

Doc quickly showed us how to steer with the reins and our legs. "Just sit back and enjoy the ride. These horses have the trail memorized and they stick to it," Doc said, adding under his breath, "except for maybe Road Rage."

The trail ride took us about an hour to complete, which was about an hour too long. My rear end was sore and getting off my horse as quickly as possible was the only thing on my mind as we came within sight of the barn.

I got Sunset back to her stall and went to brush her down when my heart lurched inside my chest.

At the barn's entrance, Mr. Snuffles swung back and forth like a wrecking ball as King Arthur gnawed away at him.

"No!" I picked up a stick and flung it at King Arthur. It smacked him on the rump, but it wasn't enough to stop him from devouring the elephant. I sprinted, grabbing the closest thing to throw—a chicken. I wadded up the mass of feathers the best I could and hurled it with such ferocity that even JT Radamoskovich would have been impressed. King Arthur took one look at the ball of angry feathers speeding toward him, dropped Mr. Snuffles, and bolted down a path. The indignant chicken clucked and walked away.

My precious elephant lay in the dirt. Part of his trunk and head, along with some of his torso, were gone. I held him close as tears pooled in my eyes. I felt foolish for crying over a stuffed animal, but I couldn't help myself.

Pogo knelt next to me and draped her arm over my shoulder. "Oh, Chloe, I'm so sorry. Maybe we can fix him?"

"Or maybe you could put it out of its misery and toss it in the trash." Victoria stood near the entrance, holding Daisy by the reins.

"Go away," Pogo said.

"Guess that wasn't the greatest hiding spot," Victoria said, not even trying to hide her smirk. "Goats are so intelligent, you know. And they're very good climbers." She moseyed down the barn corridor and put Daisy back in her stall.

Wednesday, June 16
9:21 p.m.

WORST DAY EVER—(much worse than Monday)!!!

A Ziploc bag is all that is keeping Mr. Snuffles together—I hate that goat. Mr. Snuffles was all I had left from my grandpa. I have NO DOUBT that Victoria let King Arthur out of his stall and fed him Mr. Snuffles! I hate her as much as I hate King Arthur.

I spent all afternoon crying—at least when Victoria wasn't around. It's not that I care A LOT (just a little) about what she thinks, but I know she'll only make my life more miserable if she sees me upset. Popular kids like her are like that. Nath♥n seemed clueless to the fact that I didn't eat anything at dinner and was sad. He's a good friend, but he can be pretty oblivious at times. I guess it's good he didn't notice I'd been crying—he might think I'm a crybaby.

Pogo said Mr. Snuffles can be repaired, but I

know that no amount of stuffing or stitching will be able to put him back the way he was.

A boy from the Seneca cabin, Miguel Fernandez, got the kindness award tonight. At least someone was happy. Coach Fox said it was for picking up a bunch of trash that had been blown around from a fallen trash can.

Friday, June 18
Assume Sign-Ups Will Be a Piece of Cake

• •

THE FIRST WEEK AT Camp Minnehaha flew by faster than King Arthur could roll down a hill, eat an elephant, or dodge a chicken. Pogo and I spent all our free time together. Every once in a while, we'd spy Director Mudwimple driving the camp golf cart around the grounds, sometimes with a leash in one hand and sometimes with an iced tea. I was pretty sure I knew which animal the leash was for. Even though I didn't have any more run-ins with King Arthur, there were times when bushes would move and leaves would rustle for no apparent reason, and I would grab the closest stick to defend myself.

The only break from the miserable heat we had was the cool lake. The floating dock was by far our favorite thing—mainly because of the Taco and Burrito Wars. A group of campers (usually the sports jocks) would swim the gigantic dock out to the middle of the lake, and then we'd divide into two teams, Tacos or Burritos. We spent the whole time pushing the other team off the dock. It was King of the Hill, only with Mexican food. Pogo and Sebastian always picked the Taco team. Nathan and I were always Burritos.

It was also during the first week that I confirmed I'd never be a veterinarian. In my opinion, animals were nothing but trouble. The thought of spending a week at a barn was not my idea of fun. Plus, there were way too many spiders there. And I don't mean small ones—I mean the kind that turn around and glare at you when you step on them.

Moreover, during one of the trail rides, I'd overheard Doc telling Pogo about all the math classes he took in college. Any profession with that much math was not going to float my boat.

I also discovered which horses were Footloose and Road Rage. Footloose should've been named Lose-a-Foot. He treated campers' feet the same way I wanted to treat spiders—he smashed them. He'd purposely wait for some innocent, unsuspecting person to walk up to him and then *whammo*! He'd slam his hoof down on their foot. He did it every time.

Road Rage was generally a pain in the rear end (and everywhere else for that matter). He didn't like going on trail rides. He would either try to scrape his rider off by rubbing against every tree we rode near, or he would take off down a trail until Doc could catch up, grab the reins, and lead him back to where the rest of us waited.

I just didn't see myself working with animals as a profession anytime soon…or ever for that matter.

I also ruled out any professional sport whose equipment involved a ball. I could play a decent game of HORSE back home, but at Camp Minnehaha, my special basketball moves weren't appreciated.

We had learned some awesome things from Ms. Jacqueline, but definitely not enough for Mrs. Peghiny to let me handle the cupcake portion of her ice cream parlor. I wasn't worried though—once I signed up for the cake decorating elective and had Ms. Jacqueline teaching several hours a day for a whole week, I'd be ready.

As the first week ended, our instructors took a few minutes during their sessions to tell us what we'd be doing if we chose their elective for the following week. At the science lab, Dreamy Dave, as Pogo and I secretly referred to him, got our attention by blasting music from the Beach Boys.

"Yo, check it!" he said. "Tomorrow is Saturday, and you will choose which awesome instructor you want to have for your elective. If you dudes and dudettes decide to stick to science, I guarantee a slammin' time!"

"I'm sticking here!" someone yelled.

"That's awesome, bro." Dave continued. "In the science lab, you'll work on your own experiment throughout the week. When your parents come next Saturday night, we'll put on a science extravaganza so they can see the craziness you've been up to!" He clapped his hands and rubbed them together. "Peace out!"

I summed up our choices over dinner. "The vet med people get their own animal for a week, the sports jocks will have a tournament, science does a science fair, and Ms. Jacqueline already said the cake decorating group will make the desserts for the grand finale banquet." I turned to Nathan. "Which elective are you going to take?"

"I think I'll go for the science lab. I've got an idea for an experiment."

"What is it?" I asked.

Nathan leaned back in his chair with his hands locked behind his head and grinned. "I'll tell you once I know my spot in the lab is set and we've started. I don't want anyone stealing my idea."

Sebastian chased a tomato around his plate with his fingers. "I bet your idea is not as *bueno* as mine."

Pogo turned to him. "You're doing science lab too?"

"*Si*—yes. And you?"

"I'm also picking science!" Pogo said. She seemed

extra jittery—I guess she was thinking about the sign-ups tomorrow. Her right leg started bouncing up and down and knocked the table. We all grabbed our drinks to keep them from toppling over.

"What experiment are you going to do?" I asked her.

"Don't know yet," Pogo said but then scowled. "I think I want to invent something though. Maybe a new type of lock for King Arthur's stall—that should be a piece of cake."

Sebastian looked puzzled. "You will be giving a goat a piece of cake?"

Nathan laughed. "No. 'Piece of cake' means it will be easy."

I shook my head. "That animal is a whole basket of crazy."

"*But* he is cute," Pogo said. She nibbled on a fry. "He has those floppy ears and that blank expression—it's like he always needs a hug or something."

"You mean something like a brain?" I suggested. I was still furious with him for eating Mr. Snuffles and earning me a demerit.

"Oh, don't pick on him," she said. "He's confused, that's all." She banged the underside of the table with her leg again.

I grabbed my drink. "Well, I'm going for cake decorating. Mrs. Peghiny said if I took the class and did well, she'd pay me to decorate cupcakes at the parlor—then I can buy a new bike." Since Nathan and Sebastian were from the same town as me, they knew how awesome Peghiny's Ice Cream Parlor was.

"Mmmm…I want a piece of that pie," Nathan said.

"What pie?" said Sebastian.

I shook my head. "No, Sebastian—Nathan means he wants in on the action. He probably thinks I'll sneak him some extra dessert from class, right, Nathan?" I winked.

Nathan nodded. "You know it!"

Sebastian furrowed his brow. "So there's no pie or cake?"

"Nope."

"How you say…bummer?"

"Yep, it's a bummer." I pushed my chair back and grabbed my cup. "I'm going to get more soda. Anybody else want some?"

Pogo handed me her cup. It was bouncing up and down with the rhythm of her leg.

Nathan looked from Pogo to me. "You know that's like giving a Mountain Dew to a squirrel, right?"

Pogo looked at him. "What do you mean?"

Nathan shook his head. "Never mind."

Friday, June 18
9:01 p.m.

I'm so nervous. Tomorrow we pick our electives. I HAVE to get cake decorating!!

Pogo, Nath♡n, and Sebastian all want science. Sebastian is getting confused with the English language (again). Pogo loves his accent—it is pretty cool.

I broke my hairbrush today just trying to brush my hair—I hate humidity. I had to spend the extra money Mom and Dad sent me to buy a replacement brush—I wanted candy bars.

Pogo tried to cheer me up by telling me her dad once told her there's a verse somewhere in the Bible where a man compliments his true love by telling her she has hair like a flock of goats! What kind of compliment is that?!?! My hair looks more like a flock of goats ran through it. Still... it made me laugh.

Anna is still running around doing whatever Victoria tells her to. Yesterday, she even put toothpaste on Victoria's toothbrush so it'd be ready for her when she got out of the shower.

Victoria calls Director Mudwimple "Mudpuddle"— not to her face of course! Ha-ha! She'll never win the Distinction of Recognized Kindness award if Director Mudwimple hears that.

Charlotte complained to Mindy that Marcie's snoring is keeping her up at night. For me, it's the crackling plastic bag Mr. Snuffles is in—but I still want him near me. ☺

I'll just die if I don't get my elective.

Good night.

Saturday, June 19
Make a Mess in the Mess Hall

. . . .

I HAD A PLAN to make sure my name got on the cake decorating list. I figured my best bet that morning was to sit with my friends at a table near the front doors of the mess hall, skip eating breakfast, and be ready to move fast.

So while Nathan, Sebastian, and Pogo ate their eggs and pancakes, I sipped on OJ and waited for Director Mudwimple to tell us what to do. I wouldn't have been able to eat even if I had wanted to with my stomach churning the way it was.

The anticipation of sign-ups obviously didn't have much of an effect on Nathan's and Sebastian's appetites. They were having a contest to see who could cram the most food into their mouths in a single bite. Pogo jittered in her chair, cheering on Sebastian as he finished off his last three strips of bacon.

"That was a piece of pie."

Nathan shook his head. "Dude, the saying is a 'piece of cake.'"

"Does type of pastry really matter?" Sebastian asked.

Pogo laughed at them and then turned to me. "Do you feel okay? You aren't eating."

"I'm fine. I'm just nervous about choosing our electives. Remember Mindy said cake decorating fills up fast."

"Don't worry—I'm sure we'll both get what we want." She harpooned a piece of pancake onto her fork.

Nathan slapped Sebastian a high five as he folded an entire pancake in his mouth.

I shuddered. "Why do guys think that's an accomplishment?"

"Wana-pla-tahtoh-n-barritos-witus?" Nathan mumbled.

"I can't understand you when you talk with your mouth full of food." I wrinkled my nose in disgust. "Plus, it's gross."

Nathan swallowed the pancake and washed it down with a tall glass of milk. "I said, 'Do you want to play Tacos and Burritos with us?'"

I looked at Pogo and she nodded.

"Count us in," I said, "but *after* sign-ups."

Director Mudwimple climbed onto the stage, gripping the microphone. Within moments, it was so quiet you could hear a napkin flutter to the floor. "After you're done eating, take your breakfast trays to the dish counter and unload them. The front porch is about to be pressure washed, so go out the *back* doors. There, you will find four tables, each with a sign-up sheet. Write your name under the elective you want. Your first choice may fill up right away, so please have a second option in mind."

She waited for the murmurs and whispers to stop before she continued. "If you don't get the elective you want and can find someone who is willing to trade with you, you may do so. But there will be no trading after tomorrow morning. And under no circumstances may you sign up a friend. If we see you do that, *you* will not get your elective."

Coach Fox stepped up next to her and took the mic. It was only eight thirty in the morning, and he already had sweat stains on his shirt. "Also, if you do not clean off your breakfast tray, you will not get the elective you sign up for… and we have ways of finding out who doesn't clean their tray." He stared at us silently before continuing. "You'll have free time until lunch, so we can organize classes and get prepared for you hooligans. You're dismissed." He didn't really need the mic, but I think he liked being loud.

It was every man for himself.

The frantic smacking of dishes onto trays and chairs scraping against the floor filled the mess hall. Squealing and noisy chatter got louder and campers mobbed the dish counter to stack their dirty trays before bum-rushing the back door.

I grabbed my glass. "C'mon!"

Pogo threw her silverware and cup onto her tray, seized it, and followed.

I kicked myself for picking the table closest to the *front* of the mess hall. The door to the back was already jammed with campers—I knew I needed to move fast and get back there.

I wiggled and squirmed my way through the crowd to the tray counter. Pogo was a couple feet behind me.

"Hurry!"

At least half of the campers were already stampeding out the back door. I made it to the counter and tossed my juice glass down. I turned around to look for Pogo. She'd also found a clear spot and was unloading her plates.

"Almost done!" she yelled.

I spun around and crashed into Queen Victoria. A splash of her juice landed on her white polo. She looked down at her shirt and then scowled at me. "Watch out," she sneered.

"I'm sorry," I said. "I didn't know you were right behind me."

"Just look where you're going."

I looked over her shoulder. More kids were leaving through the back.

Pogo jogged past and motioned for me to follow. "Meet you at the lake in a few minutes!"

"I gotta go, Victoria. I'm sorry I bumped you," I said, moving to the side.

She rolled her eyes at my apology.

I dodged around her, but before I could pass, her foot slipped out in front of me and I fell flat on my stomach.

"Oops," she sang.

I rolled over and looked up at her as campers stepped around me.

One corner of her mouth turned up in a smirk. "Sorry. You really should look where you're going."

I clenched my fists. More campers scurried past me to the door—I was wasting time.

"Forget about it," I said, standing up.

Her fork fell from her tray. She smiled sweetly. "Can you pretty please get that fork? My hands are full."

I rolled my eyes but bent down to pick it up.

Seconds later, orange juice, bits of pancake, maple syrup, and eggs oozed down my head and splattered on the floor.

Victoria snickered. "Oh. I. Am. So. Sorry."

I scrambled up and stared at her, heat surging through my body. "You did that on purpose!"

"Prove it." She plopped the tray on the counter and crossed her arms. "Oh, and you really should wash out that shirt. Our housekeeper says orange juice can stain if it's left on clothing too long." She gave me one last smirk, turned on her heel, and walked out the back door.

I grabbed a handful of paper napkins and wiped myself down. A kitchen assistant came around the corner and freaked out when she saw the mess. She made me help her mop up before I could go to the sign-up table. I pretended it was Victoria's perfect hair I was using to smear food across the floor instead of the dingy, old mop—it didn't make me feel any better though.

No one was left at the sign-up tables when I got there. The cake decorating list had thirty slots on it. Slot number thirty read *Victoria Radamoskovich*. She'd even had the nerve to dot her *i*'s with hearts.

Saturday, June 19
Throw a Pity Party

. . . .

I STARED AT THE four elective lists.

Three of them were full.

The only one left with an opening was veterinary medicine.

A vein in my forehead started to twitch as I stood there clenching and unclenching my fists. My chin quivered and I willed the brimming tears in my eyes not to fall. They didn't obey me and flowed down my cheeks, mixing with the dried orange juice and sticky syrup.

I scrawled my name on the last line of the vet med list and threw the pen into the bushes. I certainly didn't feel like playing Tacos and Burritos anymore. I just wanted to be alone, but I knew everyone was waiting for me by the lake. More than anything, I needed a shower—insects were beginning to buzz around me.

I trudged back to the cabin and grabbed my shower caddy and towel. Luckily, since it was free time, no one else was there to hear me cry in the shower as the events of the morning sank in. I couldn't take the cake decorating class, which meant I couldn't work for Mrs. Peghiny, which meant I couldn't earn money, which meant I couldn't buy a new bike, which meant I *was going to be* a total dorkapotamus when school started. I pictured myself wearing T-shirts with *Losers Unite* scrawled across the front and hanging out under the school bleachers with other kids whose bikes dated back to their toddlerhood.

My life was ruined—and I was only twelve.

After I got dressed, I washed my clothes out in the sink (I didn't want the orange juice stain to set) before hanging them up in a shower stall to drip dry. I sat on the edge of my bunk and reached to the bottom of my sleeping bag for Mr. Snuffles. Holding him through the Ziploc bag didn't make me feel any better. I tucked him back into the sleeping bag and left to break the news to my friends.

I found Pogo first. She was slapping sunscreen on her freckled arms as I walked up.

"Hey, why aren't you in your suit?" She squinted, either from the bright sun or from the fact that her glasses weren't on. "Your hair's wet. I know my eyesight isn't the greatest, but even I would've seen you if you'd already been swimming." She laughed at her own joke but stopped when she saw my expression. "What's wrong?"

"I didn't get cake decorating."

"What?" Her mouth flew open. She actually stopped bouncing for once. "But you were right behind me. What happened?"

"Queen Victoria happened." I filled her in on the details.

Pogo stared at me. "No!"

I nodded, and the more I told her, the redder her face became.

"Victoria Radamoskovich is such a jerk!" she stammered out. "Did you tell Coach Fox or Director Mudwimple?"

"No one was around by the time I made it out there. Plus, Victoria's right. I can't prove she did it on purpose. It'd be her word against mine."

Pogo put her arm around me and pulled me in for a hug. "I am so sorry. If I'd known about Victoria, I would have risked signing your name for you."

I scowled. "I'll get even with her. All I need is a large bowl of mashed potatoes, a squeegee, and some duct tape."

Pogo raised an eyebrow. "Not really sure how those three work together, but I'd suggest not doing anything. What goes around, comes around. You don't want to get yourself in trouble."

Nathan and Sebastian sloshed from the lake to where we stood on the pier and Pogo told them everything. Sebastian said something in Spanish. I wasn't totally sure what it was, but Pogo told me later she thought it involved a slug and some salt.

Nathan winced. "That bites."

His sympathy made me feel a little better.

"So which elective *did* you end up with?" Pogo asked.

I flopped my arms at my side. "Veterinary medicine. Maybe your invention idea of a new lock for King Arthur will come in handy—although you can bet Victoria's cupcakes I won't be choosing *him* for my animal."

Saturday, June 19
Chuck It and Hope for the Best

• • • • • • • • • • • • • • • • • • • •

SATURDAY TURNED OUT TO be the longest day ever. Why Doc thought a horseshoe tournament was a fun way to pick an animal was beyond me. We all met at the barn entrance after lunch to hear the rules of the game. I looked around the group and saw Charlotte the Busybody and Leslie the Nervous Wreck. Doc joined us, holding two giant horseshoes and wearing a smile the size of Texas. He had a metal stake in his right hand, a can of orange spray paint in his left, and a hammer jammed through his belt.

"Y'all ready for this?" he said.

We murmured something along the lines of yes. Leslie cracked her knuckles.

Doc motioned for us to follow him toward an open pasture. "Watch out for piles of you-know-what." He winked and led us to the center of the field. "Stay here."

He walked *forever* before taking out the hammer and pounding in the stake.

I looked at Charlotte. "Does he seriously expect us to fling a giant metal horseshoe that far?"

She shrugged. "I guess so. It looks like my chances of getting a horse for the week are pretty slim. Maybe I'll get the llama instead."

Whenever my family goes miniature golfing, I use a technique I call the No-Aim Swing. I whack the ball with everything I've got. It flies through waterfalls and bushes and ricochets off fake rocks and plastic gnomes; I almost always get at least one hole-in-one. Perhaps a form of the No-Aim Swing would work for horseshoes? Maybe call it the No-Aim Fling? As long as no one was standing near the stake and might get hit, it was worth a try. Things couldn't get much worse than being stuck with a bunch of animals.

"My grandparents have a farm, you know," Charlotte said, reaching down for a stick.

"Really? Where?" I asked.

"In Wisconsin." She slapped at the tall grass as we waited. "They have dairy cows."

"Cool," I said. "So do they make cheese?"

"No, cows make milk—thought you knew that," she said.

"Very funny."

Charlotte smiled. "Can't help but notice you seem a little, shall we say…tense?"

"I'm not really an animal person."

"You made an odd choice for an elective then—unless you're a *I'm going to face my fears* kinda girl. Are you?"

"Well, uh—" I said.

She flung her free arm around me. "That's great! I'm proud of you."

"But—"

She squeezed my shoulder. "Listen, I know I can come across a little bossy, and *maybe* I get involved in other people's business, but it's only because I want to help. And I am going to help you."

I tripped over a rock hidden by tall grass. "Splendid."

"What you need is accountability," she said.

"Accounting isn't really my thing. Truth be told, math and I don't get along."

"Not accounting, accountability." She threw the stick off to the side. "Someone to push you—to keep you on track."

"Oh."

"That person is going to be me," Charlotte said.

I sighed. "I'm honored."

"Okay, folks, start a line here." Doc sprayed a short line of orange paint on the ground.

We were dangerously near a cow pie that, without a

doubt, came from the world's largest cow. It blew my mind that Doc didn't seem to notice the smell.

"Here are the rules. Y'all get one chance to toss this horseshoe"—he held it up—"onto that stake twenty feet away. It's okay if you don't touch the stake; just get as close as you can. I'll record your toss, and we'll know who's got what animal faster than green grass through a goose."

I shuffled into line behind Leslie and Charlotte, at the very end.

"So what animal do you want?" Charlotte asked.

I didn't *want* any animal, yet there I was, forced to look after some critter for a whole week. I glanced at another cow pie near me and scrunched my nose. "Definitely not a cow considering Doc said we'd have to clean out their pens. Look at the size of that thing."

"Good point. I hadn't thought of that," Charlotte said.

"I don't want anything that's going to ram me, butt me, step on me, or spit on me."

"You've definitely narrowed down your options. I think that leaves you the cat, the dogs, or the chickens."

I remembered Doc said part of our responsibilities included playing with our animal. I could handle taking care of a dog. Napoleon, my neighbor's dog, was awesome at catching tennis balls. Cats were fine too. I knew they didn't play much, but that was okay. I tried to picture myself playing with chickens. What would I do? Play Duck, Duck, Goose? From what I presumed of chickens, their IQ levels were slightly higher than a pancake's. Duck, Duck, Goose would probably confuse them.

We moved ahead in line. It was going faster than I expected. Because Doc had brought two horseshoes, one was always being tossed while the other was carried back to the line by the person who last threw it.

Leslie the Nervous Wreck was now at the front. Charlotte and I stood behind her. Leslie gripped the horseshoe and swung her arm a couple times before letting loose. My mouth dropped as the horseshoe flew through the air and landed just inches from the stake.

Charlotte glanced back at me, eyes wide with disbelief. "Did you see that?"

Leslie turned and grinned at us. It was the first time since camp started that I hadn't seen her anxious.

"I bet she's going to be able to have a horse for sure," Charlotte said.

I nodded.

"Here goes nothing," Charlotte muttered, side-stepping the cow patty and swinging her arm back. The horseshoe sailed and landed a couple feet from the stake.

"Hey!" she spun around and started jumping. "That was pretty good!"

"Not bad at all," I said.

Leslie made it back to the throwing line and handed me the Horseshoe of Doom. I gripped it. It was heavier than I imagined it'd be—about the same weight as my math textbook. Math and doom have always gone together in my opinion.

I swallowed and closed my eyes. *Just chuck it and hope for the best.* I brought my arm back, took a step, and let loose with all my strength—but not before my foot landed in the cow pie and slid out from under me. My arm went over my head and the horseshoe sailed through the air—behind me.

Charlotte ducked. "Look out!"

Everyone scattered, and there I was again: the center of the wrong kind of attention.

"At least you didn't *land* in the poop," Charlotte said.

"Yeah, well, somehow that doesn't make me feel better." I got up and scraped my shoe along the grass, cleaning it off the best I could.

Doc pulled up the stake and trotted to where we all stood. "Okay, folks, I've got the results. Are y'all ready to hear 'em?"

No…I could do without hearing the results.

Saturday, June 19
Entertain a Trade

· · · · · · · · · · · · · · · · · · ·

At dinner, Victoria plopped down in the empty chair next to me.

I stopped with my burger halfway to my mouth. "What are you doing here?"

She took a sip of her soda, leaving a lip gloss smear on the straw. "It's a free country. I just thought I'd join you and see how your day on the farm went." She winked.

Pogo shot her a glare.

I shifted my chair and turned my back to Victoria.

"How'd the horseshoe tournament go?" Nathan asked me.

"About as well as it could when you slip in a pile of cow dung, fall, and throw the horseshoe *behind* you."

Nathan laughed so hard he almost fell out of his chair.

"I'd think it was funny too if I hadn't gotten stuck with that idiot goat. There I am, watching all the normal animals get chosen, one by one. The horses went first—no surprise there. No one wanted King Arthur. He was the only animal left."

"Poor King Arthur," said Pogo.

Victoria started humming "Old MacDonald Had a Farm."

I ignored her, but my face flushed anyway.

Pogo picked up her fork and harpooned a tomato. "I saw Charlotte and Leslie chose vet med too. What animals did *they* get?"

"Leslie got a horse. Charlotte got the chickens. She's named them all after dipping sauces."

Sebastian snorted. "That is funny."

"Not as funny as your science experiment," said Nathan.

"What's your experiment, Sebastian?" I asked.

Sebastian cleared his throat. "I am going to prove Spanish is the best language in the world."

"Lame," Victoria said under her breath.

I took a deep breath and counted to ten. It was something my mom told me to do whenever I got mad—although with Victoria, I might need to count a lot higher than ten.

I cleared my throat. "How are you going to prove that Spanish is better?"

"Easy," Sebastian said. "I talk to plants."

I coughed into my drink. "I don't see how talking to shrubbery is going to prove anything…except that you're nuts."

"Nuts have *nada* to do with it," Sebastian said. "I take two sets of plants. I talk to one in English and the other in

Español. The plants that grow fastest and best will be Spanish plants. Just wait, you will see." He grinned.

"What's your experiment going to be, Nathan?" I asked.

"Sea monkeys."

Victoria snickered next me. This time I counted to twenty.

"What are sea monkeys?" asked Pogo.

"They're a type of brine shrimp. Mega-tiny—you can't even see them unless you look superclose, at least when they first hatch."

"Do they actually look like monkeys?"

"No. You basically add shrimp eggs to salt water and watch them grow. Actually, Mr. Dave already has hatched sea monkeys I can use." He thought for a minute. "I think I want to experiment with what kind of food makes them grow the fastest."

I'd never heard of sea monkeys before. "What do they normally eat?"

"Yeast."

Victoria sat up straight. "Well, stay out of my kitchen—you'll have to get your yeast elsewhere."

I turned to her. "Why don't *you* stay out of our conversation, Victoria? Plus, it's not *your* kitchen."

She smirked. "Well, it's definitely not yours, Goat Girl." She leaned in and whispered, "But it could be."

I stared at her. "What's that supposed to mean?"

She stood and picked up her tray. "You want to trade jobs? Find me after everyone's asleep. And come alone."

During evening free time, Pogo and I sat on my bed playing War.

"What do you think she wants?" Pogo asked.

"Who?"

"Victoria," she said.

"I don't know," I said. "She probably wants me to do her nails or fluff her pillow each night."

"Just be careful—she doesn't seem very trustworthy."

I feigned shock. "No! Really?"

"Don't say I didn't warn you," Pogo said.

Saturday, June 19
Steal a Pair of Underwear

. . . .

I WAITED FOR LIGHTS-OUT and for everyone's breathing to sound regular and deep. Victoria slithered down from her bunk. She opened the door to the bathroom and motioned to me. I grabbed my flashlight and followed.

"So what's this all about?" I asked once the door closed.

"It's a dare. Plain and simple."

"What kind of dare? Why?"

Victoria tucked her hair behind her ear. "Mudpuddle gave me a demerit today because of a 'misunderstanding' at the camp store."

"What 'misunderstanding'?"

"I wanted a soda, so I took one." She shrugged. "Mud-puddle is making a big deal out of nothing."

"Shoplifting isn't 'nothing.'"

"I didn't shoplift," she hissed. "When she caught me, I told her to charge it to my account. My family could *buy* this camp if we wanted to."

"I guess having a brother who's rich and famous has its perks after all."

Her jaw tightened.

I sighed. "What does this have to do with trading electives?"

"I want you to sneak into Mudpuddle's cabin and take a pair of her underpants and run them up the flagpole. For the whole camp to see. And if you do this for me, I will give you my spot in the cake class."

I narrowed my eyes. "How do I know you'll keep your word?"

"Guess you'll just have to trust me."

I scoffed. "What if I get caught?"

Victoria twirled her hair around her finger. "Not my problem. But if you're successful, Mudpuddle will never know it was you. And you'll be in the cake class, so you can get your silly little bike. You're the only person desperate enough to try it."

I *was* desperate. I *needed* the cake class. I had nothing against Director Mudwimple. In fact, I kind of liked her. I was glad she had given Victoria a demerit for shoplifting. I just wish she had sent Victoria packing instead—then I could've had Victoria's spot without involving Mudwimple's underpants.

"Fine. I'll do it."

"You have to do it tonight. If her undies are flapping in the breeze tomorrow morning, we'll trade places. If not, have fun at the barn." And with that, she walked out of the bathroom.

I looked at my watch. It was 10:30 p.m. Pajamas weren't exactly ideal clothes for an undercover underwear operation, but changing would make too much noise, and I couldn't risk waking anybody. I tucked my flashlight into my pocket, slipped my shoes on, and tiptoed out the cabin door into the night.

I knew Director Mudwimple's cabin was next to the *Reg st ation Off ce*. She had mentioned it the first day, adding that her door was always open to us if we needed anything. I didn't think her open-door policy applied to stealing underwear.

It was dead quiet and kind of spooky knowing I was the only person up. The floodlights gave off an eerie, orange glow, and the moon was bright enough that, thankfully, I didn't need to use my flashlight. If anyone did happen to look outside and see a flashlight beam, I'd be caught. I sprinted across the open field toward Mudwimple's cabin. Once there, I listened for any movement inside. Blood thumping in my ears was the only sound. So much was at risk: if I got caught breaking into the director's cabin, Mudwimple would call my parents to come get me for sure. They'd have to leave their cruise, and I'd be grounded until I was eighty-five. The bike was worth the risk though. The only way to get the bike was to take the cake class, and the only way to take the cake class was to steal Mudwimple's underwear.

My sweaty hands shook as I reached for the stair rail. I didn't know if the steps were creaky, so I took a big step over them to the porch. My heart pounded harder. With two deep breaths and one turn of the knob, I slowly pushed the door open.

I stood in pitch-blackness, barely breathing, waiting for my eyes to adjust. It took only a moment to make out the sleeping form of Director Mudwimple. Thankfully, her back was to me.

Her cabin was a copycat of mine but with better carpeting. At least there'd be no creaking wooden floors. A small dresser stood against one wall. I tiptoed toward it, keeping my eyes on Mudwimple's sleeping bulk.

I gripped the small knobs of the top drawer and pulled. It didn't budge. I glanced at Mudwimple. She was still sleeping—probably dreaming of plunging into pools of iced tea. I swallowed and jerked on the knobs this time. The drawer opened a teeny bit.

Director Mudwimple snorted in her sleep and rolled over. *Please, please, please, don't open your eyes.* I held my breath and tugged a little more on the drawer. Another inch appeared. I could see inside but barely—not enough to know if I had the right drawer. I wiggled my hand down and touched fabric with my fingers. I pulled it out.

A sock.

I needed to see farther inside. I gave another tug, and without warning, the drawer sprung loose. Like a volcano shooting lava in the air, clothing spewed from the cramped and crowded box onto the floor. The dresser wobbled, and a framed photograph on top fell over. I squeezed my eyes shut and froze. I was toast—I knew it.

I was probably already a juvenile delinquent in her eyes because of the demerit. Now I was going to be caught in her cabin! Maybe I could tell Mudwimple I was sleepwalking or I thought this was *my* cabin. Better yet, that I saw an intruder and was coming to her rescue, using a dresser drawer for my weapon of choice. Yeah…that should do the trick.

But she kept sleeping.

A humongous pair of undies covered my feet. I shoved them in my back pocket, stashed everything else back inside the drawer, and gently wiggled it shut the best I could. I stood the fallen photograph up and backed out of the room. When I shut the front door, I jumped down the wooden steps and broke for the flagpole.

I had done it.

I was an underwear ninja who would be taking a cake-decorating class come tomorrow morning! Reaching the flagpole, I yanked the underpants from my pocket, knelt down, and fumbled with the clasp on the rope at the base of the pole.

"Naaa."

Startled, I looked up and stared into the eyes of King Arthur.

"Where did you come from?" I knew Victoria wasn't behind *this* escape. She was hungry for revenge like King Arthur was hungry for underpants.

"Naaaa."

"Shhhh," I whispered, glancing around.

He looked greedily at the underpants.

"These aren't for you," I told him.

He gave me a look that said, *They aren't for you either.* I stood up and brushed off my knees with the underwear.

Without warning, he ripped them from my hand. Director Mudwimple's undies hung from King Arthur's mouth.

"Give those back," I whispered, making a grab for them. He dodged my hand and backed up a few feet.

"Come here, boy," I coaxed.

He took a step closer, and I snatched them. His jaws clamped tight, and we started a round of tug-o'-war with

Director Mudwimple's underpants. Round one went to me as I gained more fabric. Round two started in my favor, but he nibbled and tugged inches of underwear from my grasp. With a determined yank from King Arthur followed by a loud rip, I fell onto my butt and was left holding a small, mangled patch of white. Everything else hung from King Arthur's mouth. He turned and ran away with his stolen booty.

I stood and brushed myself off.

"Miss McCorkle, what are you doing out of your cabin?"

I spun around, coming face-to-face with Director Mudwimple. My mouth went dry. I shoved the patch of underwear into my back pocket.

"Uh...I...um...I couldn't sleep. I thought I would go for a walk?" I stammered and crossed my fingers.

"I understand not being able to sleep. I myself thought I heard something and came to investigate. But under no circumstances are campers allowed out at night, especially to go on a walk! I'm afraid this blatant disregard for the rules, which were clearly outlined in our welcome folder, has earned you a demerit. Please return to your cabin immediately, and let's not have any more nighttime walks."

"Yes, ma'am."

A couple minutes later, I kicked off my shoes and climbed into bed. Victoria was asleep with the rest of the world, probably dreaming about Director Mudwimple's underpants on a flagpole. But when she woke up, she'd discover they were not there. She won't have gotten her revenge, and I won't have gotten the cake class.

Saturday, June 19
11:30 p.m.

WORST DAY EVER!!! (I'm not kidding.)

Victoria thinks just because she's rich or something that she can have whatever she wants. She's a food-dumping, lying, pain-in-the-rear brat—who also shoplifts!

And now I'm permanently stuck with that walking garbage disposal King Arthur! Not only does he eat adorable stuffed animals, but he also ate Director Mudwimple's underpants! Don't ask. He has serious issues. I am making it my personal mission to discover how he gets out all the time!

I got another demerit tonight—for being out of my cabin at night. Luckily, Director Mudwimple doesn't know about her underwear.

All of this mess for a cake decorating class! On my way back to the cabin, I thought of a NEW plan though... I'm going to ask Ms. Jacqueline for private lessons. Between everything she taught us last week and with a private lesson or two, maybe she'll think I know enough to give me a letter of recommendation or something for Mrs. Peghiny.

IT'S PERFECT—nothing can go wrong with it (because it has nothing to do with Victoria or stupid King Arthur)!!

Sunday, June 20
Forget to Lock the Gate

. . . .

AT BREAKFAST THE NEXT morning, Victoria made eye contact with me and shook her head. *Loser,* she mouthed from across the mess hall.

Pogo sat next to me and peeled a banana. She nodded her head toward Victoria. "So what did she want you to do anyway?"

I pretended like I didn't hear.

"Chloe!"

"Hmm?"

"C'mon, I'm right next to you. It's not that loud in here."

I waved my hand dismissively. "She wanted me to... uhh—"

Nathan and Sebastian walked through the mess hall doors.

"—hook her up with Nathan."

Pogo busted out laughing. "Seriously?"

"Yeah," I scoffed. "I would rather kiss King Arthur full on the lips than do that to Nathan."

Pogo laughed. "Would you mind if I arranged that for you?"

I stirred my Frosted O's around my bowl and felt sorry for myself. I had committed a crime of breaking and entering, just so I could take Victoria's place in class, and I had nothing to show for it. And I just lied to my friend about it.

After breakfast, Pogo, Nathan, and Sebastian rushed off to the science lab, and Charlotte and I walked to the barn. We stopped near the chicken coop, watching Charlotte's chickens peck at invisible objects in the dirt.

"Well? What are you waiting for?" Charlotte said. "King Arthur's pen isn't going to clean itself, you know."

"I can't. I just can't go in there. Have you *seen* all the spiders? It's like they've tripled in number since the first day."

"It's not that bad. I know you have this thing about spiders," Charlotte said, "but they're just daddy longlegs. My little brother told me when you rub the belly of a daddy longlegs, it smells like bubble gum. You should try it—maybe it'll help you get over your fear of spiders."

I glared at her.

"Okay, fine." She smiled. "Do you want me to go in with you?"

I puffed my cheeks out. "Thanks, but I might as well get used to it, since I'm stuck with that animal all week." I turned away from the coop and started toward the barn. I called over my shoulder. "I'll just grab a broom and sweep out the webs the best I can."

Charlotte jogged to catch up with me. "There isn't much left of the broom. Someone left it a little too close to King Arthur's pen yesterday and he ate most of it."

"Figures," I said. "That goat is more trouble than he's worth."

The broom was just a tiny handful of chewed-up bristles attached to an equally gnawed-on wooded handle. It reminded me of the time my friend Jireh's little brother cut the hair on one of her Barbie dolls. I picked up the broom—or rather what was left of it.

"Stupid goat," I muttered.

Charlotte walked over to where King Arthur stood in his pen, mindlessly nibbling his way through a pile of hay. She leaned over the gate and rubbed his head. Near the front of the barn, someone started up the lawn tractor, the engine roaring to life. King Arthur jumped and fell right over in a faint.

Charlotte snorted.

"Oh brother," I said. I fumbled with the gate lock. But before I could get it open, King Arthur stood, shook himself, and went straight back to eating. "Wow, Doc wasn't kidding when he said their faint only lasts for about ten seconds."

"Have fun with that animal of mass destruction," Charlotte said. "I'm headed back out to clean the McNugget coop."

"Okay, let me know if you need help with anything."

I stuck King Arthur in his paddock; then, using the broom, I swept every inch, from the top of the wall to bottom, clearing away any cobwebs. I saved the grossest thing for last—the goat poo. That couldn't be swept. It needed to be shoveled into a bucket and taken outside to a special poop trailer. Once it's full, it's attached to a tractor and the poop can be spread evenly in the pastures as fertilizer. I took the broom back to the supply wall and hung it up. When I turned around, I ran into Leslie.

"Hey, how's your horse this morning?" I asked.

"She's great. I just groomed her, and I'm about to muck out her stall." She grabbed a lead rope from the wall. "We're supposed to put them in the west pasture, right?"

I shrugged. "I don't know. I put King Arthur in his paddock while I swept out cobwebs." I picked up a shovel and bucket. "After I de-poo his stall, I'll move him back inside and then de-poo the paddock."

Leslie scrunched her nose. "Yeah, at least his poo is small. I'm not looking forward to cleaning out Sunset's stall."

"Trust me, small poo is the *only* bonus."

I went back to King Arthur's stall. After fifteen min-utes of maneuvering my way through the land mines of poop, I decided even Doc would approve. I dragged the full bucket out of the stall to the poop trailer and dumped it. I took my time—I was in no hurry to get back to His Royal Poopiness. When I eventually made it to his stall, I stopped dead in my tracks.

The paddock gate was ajar. King Arthur was nowhere in sight.

Charlotte walked by holding a chicken, cooing to it.

"Have you seen him?" I said.

"Who?"

"King Arthur!" I ran my hand through my hair. "What am I going to do? I can't lose the goat on my first day as his caretaker!"

"Does Doc know?"

I shook my head. "Maybe I can find King Arthur be-fore anyone notices."

I grabbed two lead ropes hanging on his door and shoved one into Charlotte's chicken-free hand.

"Please, please, please help me find him," I begged.

"Let me put Barbecue away first."

"You go that way," I said, pushing her toward one end of the barn, "and I'll go this way. If you find him, use the rope and bring him back. If anyone sees you, tell them you're taking him out for a walk."

"Do people walk goats?"

"Does it matter? Just go!"

I turned and headed toward the campfire area. I didn't see him there or at the nurse's station, the *Reg st ation Off ce*, or the mess hall. Hopefully, he wasn't climbing around in the ravine—Doc did say that goats love to climb. Since we weren't allowed near there, I decided I would check the ravine as a last resort. I walked down toward the cake decorating kitchen and the lake.

"Naa."

King Arthur! He sounded far away—and not happy.

I looked around. The sun glistened off the lake and blinded me—but not before I saw him.

In the middle of the lake.

Sunday, June 20
Row, Row, Row Your Goat

. . . .

"NAA! NAAA!"

King Arthur had eaten through the rope that kept the floating dock tied to the pier. To complicate things, he was still on the dock and was now *stranded* in the middle of Lake Minnehaha.

I could run back to the kitchen to tell Ms. Jacqueline, but what could she do about it? She was petite and dainty and could no more rescue a goat from the middle of a lake than she could win an arm wrestling match against Coach Fox. There was Coach Fox, but he'd be at the playing fields. The barn was too far away for me to get Doc Mulholland—and I didn't know if goats could swim. What if King Arthur got so scared he fainted and fell off the dock and drowned while I was away getting help? Actually, my life would be a lot easier if he did fall off and drown. Maybe everyone would feel so sorry for me that they'd let me pick any elective I wanted—even if it was already full.

Or…they'd all blame me for his death, I'd be charged with murder, and go to prison for the rest of my life. Better to rescue the idiot goat than spend my life in prison.

"Naa!"

He sounded pitiful, all alone in the middle of the lake. I tossed my hands up in surrender, walked over to where the life vests hung, and grabbed a couple. I wasn't sure if he'd wear the life vest (or how I'd even get one on him), but I didn't want him to drown if he fell in.

"You'd better appreciate this," I muttered, climbing into a canoe. The canoe glided across the lake as I paddled for the dock. Moments later, I pulled up alongside King Arthur. He clip-clopped over to the edge of the dock and looked down at me.

"Naa." His eyes were huge and all four of his legs were spread wide to help him keep his balance. The dock rocked back and forth.

"Stay calm—please don't faint," I begged.

With one hand, I grabbed the dock and slowly stood in the canoe. "Come here, boy, come on," I coaxed. "The only way you're getting back to the barn is if you get in the canoe."

I tried several times to get him to jump into the canoe with me before giving up.

"Okay, it looks like we're going to have to do this the hard way."

I bent down and grabbed the floating, chewed-up rope that was still attached to the floating dock and tied it in a knot around my seat. The dock was too heavy for me to tow back to land. Plus, King Arthur might fall off once the dock started moving. When I was sure the dock and my canoe were firmly attached, I looked around to make sure no one was watching. I leaned in as close as I could to him.

"Boo!" I yelled.

He passed out.

Mission accomplished.

I knew I only had a few seconds to work. I quickly wrapped my arms around his stout body and pulled him off the dock and into the canoe with me. He was way lighter than I expected.

I clipped the lead rope to his collar, and I was even able to put the life vest around his neck before he stood up. I buckled it the best I could, but having never performed a water rescue on a demented goat before, I could've missed a vital step.

I hoped not.

"Don't move," I told him. I don't know why I was giving him instructions. I knew he couldn't understand me.

I carefully untied the rope from my seat and picked up the paddle. I pushed away from the dock and, moving slowly so I wouldn't upset King Arthur, dipped the paddle into the water. I paddled at the pace of a snail through cement, but at least we made progress. He stood in the middle of the canoe facing me, with his trademark blank expression, mindlessly nibbling the end of his life jacket, while I rowed him toward land. The whole scene reminded me of one of those old-fashioned paintings—a young man rowing a boat with a pretty lady holding a parasol, only instead, this was a goat wearing (and eating) a life jacket. About halfway to the shoreline, King Arthur started to sway from side to side as if he was ill.

Just what I needed—a seasick goat.

"Easy there, Your Highness," I said, hoping the sound of my voice would calm him. Instead, he got all twitchy and began to rock the canoe even faster. I dropped the paddle into the lake and grabbed the sides of the canoe with both hands. "Whoa! Stop moving!"

We were about twenty feet from shore. Even without the paddle, we probably could coast in if he would just hold still. King Arthur must have seen how close we were to land, because the next thing I knew, he leaped overboard, flipping me out of the canoe and into the lake.

I came up for a breath as King Arthur's life vest floated past. I grabbed it and turned in a circle, looking for the goat. Had he drowned? Finally, I saw him.

King Arthur had made it to shore and was shaking himself dry. The canoe seemed to have righted itself after I flipped out and was floating a couple feet away. I swam over and flung King Arthur's vest into it. I dragged myself out of the water, feeling ten pounds heavier than before I got wet. Hauling the canoe out of the lake, I glared at King Arthur as water dripped from my face. I swear, he grinned at me.

"Thanks for nothing, pal," I sneered.

"Naaa."

I sloshed my way over to him and picked up the wet lead rope. Babysitting would be a piece of cake compared to this.

"Let's go," I said, pulling him toward the path that led back to the barn.

Just then, Nathan rounded the corner and jerked to a stop when he saw us.

"Chloe?"

"Yes?" I tried to act normal, like I wasn't soaking wet and there wasn't a soggy goat dripping next to me.

"Uh, why are you and King Arthur both wet?"

"We went for a swim."

"Just now?"

"Yes, we couldn't do it earlier because he had finished breakfast. I heard you should always wait at least an hour after eating before swimming with a goat."

Nathan stood speechless.

King Arthur ate a flower.

I felt like an idiot.

Sunday, June 20
Put a Plan into Action

. . . .

I CAUGHT UP WITH Pogo during afternoon free time. We hung out on the pier instead of playing Tacos and Burritos. I'd had enough swimming to last the rest of the week.

As we leaned over the railing and dropped pine needles in the water, I filled her in on the morning's drama.

"I'm really sorry all that happened," she said, "but I sure wish I could have seen you scare the bejeebers out of King Arthur just to get him in the canoe."

"It was the only thing I could think of. That stupid goat made me look like a complete fool in front of—" I stopped. My crush did not need to become public knowledge.

"In front of who?" Pogo teased. "Anyone in particular?"

I blushed and shrugged. "I was on the beach in broad daylight—the whole camp could have seen for all I know."

Victoria's shrill voice carried from the canoes on the beach. She sat in the front of one as Anna struggled to shove off into the water. Eventually, she dislodged it from the sand and jumped in, sending the canoe into a teeter-totter rhythm.

"Watch it, Anna!" Victoria snapped.

"Sorry," Anna said, and paddled toward the far side of the lake.

"Why does Anna put up with her anyway?" I said.

"I don't know—maybe she's too shy to speak up for herself." Pogo dropped a handful of pine needles into the water. "If I didn't have you for a friend and I had to deal with Her Highness by myself, camp would be horrible."

The unspoken but understood rule at camp was *make friends or be a loner.* Pogo was the closest thing I had to a best friend here.

She turned to me. "I've got an awesome idea to help keep track of King Arthur."

"Glue his hooves to the barn floor? Mount his head to a wall? I'm in!"

She rolled her eyes. "No—I'm making a tracking device you can put on his collar."

"You know how to do that?"

"Yeah—I think so. My dad's an electronic engineer and our house is full of gadgets and wires and transmitters—you name it, it's there. Before Mom died, Dad and I would go on daddy-daughter dates while Mom watched my brothers and sisters. But after she died, getting a babysitter was too expensive, so instead, once my little brothers and sisters were in bed, Dad and I would go into the garage and build stuff together. He's shown me how to make lots of fun junk, and I think with stuff in the science lab, plus my cell phone, I can do it." She pushed off from the rail and smiled. "That's what my science project is—only I hope I can finish it early, so you can use it."

"That'll be supercool if it works. I'm impressed."

"Thanks."

I told Pogo I'd catch her later and headed off to find Ms. Jacqueline. It was time to put my new plan into action.

I climbed the steps to the cake kitchen and knocked on the door.

"*Oui*, come in," said Ms. Jacqueline.

I bounced inside and saw Doc Mulholland standing close to Ms. Jacqueline as she stirred something inside a pot on the stove.

"Hi, Doc. Hi, Ms. Jacqueline."

"Hi, yourself," Doc said. "I'll see you later, Jackie. Save me some of that custard."

Ms. Jacqueline laughed and waved him off. "Miss Chloe." She smiled. "What can I do for you?"

"I need to talk to you about something important."

She nodded. Her timer on the stove dinged. "Well, zen." She turned the stove off, removed the pan of custard she had been stirring, and handed me a stool. "Have a seat."

"Thanks."

I took a deep breath and swallowed. Then I opened my mouth and started talking. Before I knew it, I poured out everything about wanting a new bike, needing to earn money, and the deal I'd made with Mrs. Peghiny. I finished by saying, "So you see, I can't decorate cupcakes for Mrs. Peghiny because I wasn't able to take your class." I sighed. "I'm going to be such a dork riding my old bike to school this year."

Ms. Jacqueline let out a light laugh and placed a comforting hand on my shoulder. "A bike does not make one dorky, as you put it. Caring much of what others think of you is a big burden, *cheri*. When someone carries such burdens, they soon start making choices and acting in ways zat can make them dorky though."

"I get that. Really I do, but I think riding a new bike would be one less burden *I'd* be carrying. I'll do anything, give up whatever I need to, but, please, please, please, do you have any time when you could give me a private lesson or two? That way I could still go back home and work for Mrs. Peghiny."

Ms. Jacqueline stared thoughtfully at me for a minute

or two before answering. "My week—it is full, no? Especially with zee grand finale banquet coming up so soon."

My shoulders dropped. This was the only thing I could think of—my one and only shot.

"But I tell you what. You will have to give up your free time in zee evening, but I can give you two hours after dinner on Friday. *Bon?* Zat is the only time I have. You mustn't be late. I cannot reschedule you."

I jumped up and squealed. "Oh thank you, thank you! I won't miss it—I promise! Thank you so much!" I wrapped my arms around her and squeezed.

"You are welcome, my dear. But make sure you fulfill all your other responsibilities—I hear you have zat rascal King Arthur."

"Yeah, he's keeping me on my toes." (And in canoes and lakes.)

She smiled and gave another light laugh. "*Oui*, he is one of Doc's favorites though. He has a soft spot for zee little goat. He is very sweet."

I didn't know if she was talking about Doc or King Arthur, so I just nodded.

"Thank you again, Ms. Jacqueline. I'll see you Friday night—I will definitely be here. Even King Arthur won't keep me away."

I was getting cake lessons now that Ms. Jacqueline had agreed to help me—and it didn't involve hanging anyone's underwear on a flagpole.

Sunday, June 20
10:01 p.m.

Where do I begin?

Today was the first (and hopefully last) time
I ever swam with a goat. Stupid King Arthur—
that's his full name—not King Arthur. STUPID
KING ARTHUR.

I thought goats smelled bad to begin with, but a wet
goat stinks even worse! Doc said I was taking such
good care of King Arthur when he found me giving him
a bath. Oh well. What he doesn't know won't hurt him.

The ONLY good thing that happened was Ms.
Jacqueline agreed to give me a cake decorating
lesson Friday night. I just have to give up my free
time in the evening, but that's a sacrifice I'm
totally willing to make.

I told Pogo that Ms. Jacqueline is going to give
me lessons. She is excited for me. She's a great
friend and really sweet—I'm glad we're friends. ☺

Good night.

PS Sebastian got the Distinction of Recognized Kindness award! Dreamy Dave said it was for putting aside his own science project to help another cabin mate with theirs. Personally, I bet Dreamy Dave was just glad not to hear Sebastian yell at shrubbery. He gets loud when he speaks Spanish. It was a win-win for both.

Monday, June 21
Let Victoria Take a Walk in the Woods

. . . .

MONDAY MORNING HELD NO surprises except for the fact that King Arthur was where I last left him—in his stall. I'm sure it was a first. Our veterinary medicine group spent a couple hours taking care of our animals and learning about animal husbandry, which, as it turns out, has nothing to do with being married.

Midway through our lesson, Victoria showed up to collect the eggs for the cake kitchen. Charlotte was in the restroom, so Doc asked me to help.

Victoria stood several feet away from the coop and pranced around every time a chicken got close to her. "I'm not going in that nasty coop. It looks like something your gross elephant belongs in." Barbecue, Ranch, and Sweet 'n' Sour seemed particularly interested in her shoelaces and followed her every step.

"They're just chickens. They're not going to hurt you." I went in alone, watching carefully for spiders, and quickly filled Victoria's basket with eggs.

"I'm sure they carry diseases," she called to me from outside the coop. "Like chicken pox."

Along with teaching us animal care, Doc had also taught us a little about animal diseases.

"You can't get chicken pox from a chicken—it's only called chicken pox because the rash looks like peck marks." I shoved the basket of eggs into her hands.

"What's the quickest way out of this stinking place?" she huffed. Without waiting for an answer, she headed for the path that ran around behind the coop.

"Uh, Victoria…" I said, pointing to the path. "I don't think—"

"I don't care what you think," she said, turning on her heel and marching through the knee-high plants down the path. Right past the NO TRESPASSING sign.

I shrugged my shoulders. "Suit yourself."

In the late afternoon, as I was putting fresh wood shavings in King Arthur's stall, Doc popped his head around the door and said Director Mudwimple wanted to see me in her office.

Immediately.

A pit formed in my stomach. Maybe Director

Mudwimple realized she was missing a massive pair of underpants and put two and two together about Saturday night. Or maybe she'd found out that I'd purposely been flushing toilets during Victoria's shower. With two demerits to my name already, I had to watch out. Each step toward Mudwimple's office brought new guilt to mind.

The office door was the only thing between me and Director Mudwimple. I swallowed and knocked.

"Come in," Director Mudwimple said.

A splotchy, puffy Victoria, who, for once, did not look like a perfectly polished princess, glowered from across the room.

"You are so busted," Victoria seethed.

"I'll handle this, Victoria," Director Mudwimple said, motioning me to sit.

I couldn't peel my eyes away from the sight of Victoria, who was madly scratching. An ugly, red rash covered her legs and arms, and she had patches of it forming on her face. Poison ivy.

Director Mudwimple clapped her hands and startled me. "Miss McCorkle, Victoria tells me you purposely sent her down a path that you knew was covered with poison ivy simply because she got the last cake decorating slot."

"No, ma'am!" I gasped, shaking my head. "I tried to

tell her *not* to go down that path—but she wouldn't listen. I promise!" I stumbled my way through the morning's event, trying to remember word for word what I'd said to Victoria. If Director Mudwimple thought I sent Victoria through poison ivy on purpose, I would get a demerit for sure!

Director Mudwimple turned to Victoria. "Is that true? Did she tell you not to use that path?"

Victoria rolled her eyes and scratched her cheek.

Director Mudwimple looked over her spectacles at Victoria. "Quit scratching, dear. You'll make it worse. If Chloe tried to warn you and you didn't listen—"

"She could have tried harder to stop me."

Director Mudwimple met Victoria's gaze and didn't look away until Victoria squirmed and looked to the floor. I hoped Mudwimple saw Victoria for what she really was—a spoiled, self-centered, spiteful camper. Maybe Director Mudwimple was on Team Chloe! Solidarity, that's what it's all about—that and the hokey pokey.

"Victoria, I think you need to apologize to Chloe for your accusation."

I thought Victoria's face couldn't become any redder, what with the poison ivy rash all over it, but I was wrong. I think steam even shot from her ears. Through a clenched jaw, Victoria hissed an apology. Even though it was totally *not* sincere, I took it. Better than nothing. And now at least Mudwimple was onto her.

"I suggest you revisit the nurse's station, Victoria, and get more itch cream," Director Mudwimple said.

I stood to leave.

"Chloe, I would like you to stay, please. I want to talk to you for a moment."

I stepped aside to avoid touching Victoria as she stomped past me, seething and muttering something unintelligible. The last thing I needed was poison ivy. I jumped as the door slammed behind her.

Director Mudwimple strummed her chubby fingers on her desk. "Have a seat again, Miss McCorkle. We have another issue to discuss."

I mentally ticked off *my current* issues:

- I was a dork.
- Victoria hated me.
- King Arthur hated me.
- Mr. Snuffles had been eaten.
- I was earning demerits faster than
  a highly motivated Girl Scout was
  sewing badges to a vest.

I really wasn't sure which of those she was referring to. "Which issue? If you mean the poison ivy, I bet a healthy dose of weed killer on the path will take care of that."

Director Mudwimple shook her head. "I do *not* mean the poison ivy."

She shuffled through some papers and picked up a familiar pink form. *Disciplinary Action Report.* I gulped. The underwear!

She cleared her throat. "Victoria's frustration with you is not confined only to poison ivy. It seems you are also flushing toilets every time she showers."

Okay, it wasn't about the underwear. I put my hands up in defense. "I'm only cleaning them—she's the one who made the chore list. I've had bathroom detail *every* day. Isn't there some rule against that?"

"We all have to work together to keep our camp looking nice. I want the flushing to stop. Understand?"

"Yes." I stood.

"We're not done, Miss McCorkle."

I ran my hand over my face and sat back in my chair.

Director Mudwimple stared me down. "Apparently, our first talk involving animal cruelty and trash cans had no effect on you."

"What do you mean?"

"You hurled a chicken at King Arthur! She's so upset she's molting!"

I dropped my chin to my chest. "I do feel bad about that."

Director Mudwimple nodded. "King Arthur was dreadfully upset as well."

"I was referring to the chicken," I said under my breath.

"Miss McCorkle!" Director Mudwimple's cheeks were bright red. "And then you tried to drown that poor little goat in the lake!"

"I didn't try to drown him," I said, my voice rising. I closed my eyes and took a deep breath. "I was trying to save him. He ate through the rope that keeps the dock tied to the pier and floated himself out to the middle of the lake. I grabbed a life jacket and canoe to bring him back to shore. Halfway across the lake, he got crazy. I didn't tip the canoe on purpose. I promise."

"Hmmfph."

"The life jacket proves I was trying to help." I thought for a second and shrugged. "Actually, he ate most of it before the canoe tipped."

Director Mudwimple stared at me like I'd just told her I was a fairy princess who ruled over a great kingdom of singing oysters. "Miss McCorkle, I am giving you another demerit for your actions—be glad it's not more than one.

Your lack of compassion for King Arthur and your fellow campers is most distressing." She tidied the papers in front of her. "It may be against my better judgment that I am not removing King Arthur from your care, but I think you may be able to learn something from him, given time."

I stared at her as though she just told me I could learn something from a deranged goat.

Oh, wait…she *did* tell me that.

Monday, June 21
Start a Food Fight

. . . .

VICTORIA WALKED BY AND paused at our table at dinner that
evening. "Well, if it isn't Goat Girl," she said with a smirk.
"How's that animal working out for you?"

"How's that poison ivy working out for *you*?" I said.
"The rash still looks bad."

"Nothing a little makeup can't handle."

"I'm pretty sure you shouldn't wear makeup if you have
poison ivy on your face," said Pogo. "But maybe you could
ask your mom to send you something from Europe—the
stuff over there is more natural anyway."

I looked at Pogo. I couldn't tell if she was making fun of
Victoria's constant comments about her mom being in Europe
or just trying to be helpful. Pogo was a genuinely helpful, nice
person, so she was probably making a good suggestion.

Victoria sneered at her. "Well." She adjusted the tray in
her hands to scratch her neck and leaned in. "At least *I* have
a mom."

Our table went dead quiet. Pogo's mouth fell open. Nathan dropped his fork, and Sebastian stared at Victoria as he slowly slid his chair back. He probably would've started hurling one insult after another in Spanish, but at that exact point, I squeezed the ketchup bottle with such force that the ketchup shot a fry straight off my plate and onto Victoria.

And I kept squeezing the bottle.

All over Victoria's face.

And I remember Victoria howling like a big baby.

Oh, and Victoria's plate of mac and cheese somehow ended up on my head.

We both were sent to Director Mudwimple's office.

"Sit!" Director Mudwimple's tone undoubtedly turned her sweet tea into cough syrup.

Victoria plopped onto the metal folding chair and immediately slid off—apparently ketchup is slippery. I, on the other hand, stuck to my chair. But then again, macaroni and cheese is a starch.

"Perhaps one of you can explain what on earth happened! You were both just in here this afternoon!" Director Mudwimple barked. Clearly, she was more than a little perturbed. Her face was bright red, but I was willing to bet it had nothing to do with running around or the heat of the evening.

"She started it!" Victoria said, pointing at me.

"Did not!"

I was going to keep Pogo's name out of this. I didn't want Director Mudwimple to think she was involved and give her a demerit. She'd been a little too demerit-happy lately. "It was an accident. The ketchup bottle was jammed—sort of."

"I don't care who started it. Food fights in the mess hall, or anywhere else for that matter, are prohibited. You will both be on kitchen patrol for the next three days. And you each have *another* demerit."

Victoria gasped.

Director Mudwimple shuffled around some papers on her desk until she found her clipboard. She glanced down. "Victoria, you will have the after-breakfast shift, and, Chloe, you will take the after-lunch shift." She tossed the clipboard back onto her desk and peered over her spectacles at us. "Understand?"

I slouched in my chair. "Yes, ma'am," I muttered.

Director Mudwimple sighed. "You owe each other an apology."

Victoria opened her mouth in protest, but Director Mudwimple held up her hand in silence. "Like I said earlier, Victoria, it doesn't matter who started it. I think you two need to have a long talk with each other. This incident is finished, and we're going to forgive and move on."

"Sorry, Victoria," I said flatly.

She rolled her eyes. "Me too."

Director Mudwimple stood and opened the door to her office. "Now please get yourselves cleaned up."

Victoria stomped out the door. Director Mudwimple tapped me on the shoulder as I followed. "Chloe," she said, then looked at her hand and wiped it off on a napkin before continuing. "Mindy, tells me your bed is near Victoria's. I want you to move to a different bunk."

My shoulders dropped. "Do I have to?"

"I think it's best if you and Victoria gave each other some space—at least for the next couple days. Your cabin's not full—there's room for the change."

"Can't you just move Victoria to a different cabin?" I pleaded.

Director Mudwimple folded her hands and rested them on her desk. "I could, but I am of the belief that we should fix our problems, not run away from them."

Running away from problems seemed like a perfectly good option to me, but arguing was pointless—adults always won arguments. "Yes, ma'am."

"And, Chloe?"

"Yes?"

"Be careful. You're at four demerits—and in record time I might add."

I decided to shower before moving my things over—I didn't want to be dropping chunks of mac and cheese into my sleeping bag or suitcase. By the time I got clean and into my pajamas, brushed my teeth, and dried my hair, the lights were already out in the cabin. I felt my way to my bed and gathered up my sleeping bag and pillow. Then, I made my way to the empty bunk near Mindy's bed, stubbing my toe on Victoria's dumb makeup box in the process. I flicked on my flashlight and went back for my suitcase.

I reached down to the bottom of my sleeping bag for Mr. Snuffles and brought him up, along with my journal. I held him close, grateful he was with me.

Monday, June 21
8:54 p.m.

WORST DAY EVER!!!! (and I mean it this time)

Camp Minne-BOO-HOO is dumb and Victoria is the
WORLD'S BIGGEST DRAMA QUEEN!

How many things can go wrong in one day? I mean
SERIOUSLY!?!?!?

Things that went wrong today:

#1 Victoria got poison ivy and blamed me.

#2 Director Mudwimple found out about the
chicken I hurled at King Arthur. She gave me
another demerit. At least she doesn't know about
the underwear...yet.

#3 I got in a food fight with Victoria after she
said something horrible to Pogo. I got another
demerit, but THIS ONE was worth it. I guess
I'm at four demerits!!

At this rate, I don't know if I'll make it through camp without being kicked out. I've never been kicked out of anything before (except for that time in Girl Scouts). I would die multiple deaths of embarrassment.

I can't believe Nath♥n saw me with mac and cheese all over my head. I am so embarrassed! If he didn't think I was dork after the whole swimming with a goat incident, I'm sure he does now, after the food fight with Victoria. Ugh!

Sebastian and Nath♥n were both saying how wicked smart Pogo is with science. She was showing Dreamy Dave something with transistors, and even he was impressed. I feel really bad that I lied to Pogo about Victoria wanting me to hook her up with Nath♥n. But if I tell Pogo about sneaking into Mudwimple's cabin, she might think I'm a thief (which I am ☹).

'Night.

PS On a side note, when King Arthur does kick the

bucket, he'd look great hanging on the wall in the Registration Office next to the llama.

PPS The kindness award went to Callie Morse. She's in the vet med group with me. She got it because she offered to clean out a horse stall for Leslie, who wasn't feeling well. Considering the size of horse poop, I'd have given her the award too!

PPPS I saw Ms. Jacqueline and Doc Mulholland kiss today! She brought a plate of cookies up to the barn, and he kissed her—on the LIPS!! He was hanging out with her in the kitchen too—they are always together.

Thursday, June 24
Pour Yourself a Glass of Sea Monkeys

. . . .

BY MY THIRD DAY of kitchen patrol, I realized dish-washing duty would've been a better definition. After lunch, I went behind the serving counter and loaded Hobart—the ginormous dishwasher the size of an elephant. To keep my clothes dry, I wore a bright-yellow apron that was rubbery and heavy.

I was almost done loading the last rack when Ms. Jacqueline came into the kitchen and filled her arms with various ingredients to haul down to her kitchen.

"Ms. Chloe, before you go to your duties at the barn, would you mind please bringing zat five-gallon tub of chocolate frosting that's in zee walk-in refrigerator? My hands are full, and we will need it for zee cakes we are making today."

I nodded. "Sure. I'm almost done here."

"*C'est excellent!* Be careful; it is very heavy. You might want to use zee dolly to roll it down. By zee way, I am looking forward greatly to our lesson on Friday."

I smiled. "Me too!" I would gladly cart twenty tubs of chocolate frosting down Mess Hall Hill for Ms. Jacqueline if she wanted me to.

By the time I finished, all the other kitchen helpers had gone to their afternoon electives. Despite the fact I had been surrounded by water for the last hour, I was dying of thirst. I grabbed a clean glass and walked to the counter near the cook's office. Earlier, I had noticed she kept a pitcher of water there. I poured myself a full glass and gulped it down. It tasted funny, but I was hot and sweaty and didn't care.

The steam from Hobart had turned my hair into a frizzy style I thought could only be achieved if I stuck a fork into an electric socket. A mirror hung on the wall above the counter, and my reflection could've turned Medusa to stone. I gathered my hair up into a ponytail and was securing it with a hair tie when Nathan walked in.

"Hey," he said. "You look hot."

Act cool.

"Ha-ha," I said.

He winked. "How was KP duty?"

"Well, I get a lot of time to myself and an hour-long steam facial each day. What more could a girl ask for?"

"For what it's worth, I think Victoria had a face full of

ketchup coming the other night. If you hadn't squirted her, I sure would have. She's a creep."

Be still my heart. "Thanks, but I didn't mean to squirt the ketchup on her—at first. I just didn't realize how angry I was getting, and then"—I shrugged my shoulders—"I couldn't *stop* squeezing it."

He chuckled.

"What are you doing here, anyway?" I asked. "Aren't you supposed to be in the science lab, working on your experiment?"

"I had to get away from Sebastian. Everywhere I go, I hear him shouting at shrubbery. Besides, I needed to check on my sea monkeys." He gestured toward the back.

"Your sea monkeys are here in the kitchen? Isn't that against some food safety rule?"

"They're not in the actual kitchen. Cook said I could keep the ones who are being fed hard-boiled eggs near her office. Since the fridge in the science lab is broken, I have to keep their food up here. I just bring my clipboard and make notes."

"Oh. So what have you discovered so far? Do they grow faster with the yeast or the eggs?"

"It's still kinda hard to tell," he said, looking down at his notes. "They're so small, and I haven't compared them side by side yet. Wanna see them?"

"Sure!"

I followed him to the back of the kitchen, near Cook's office. He stopped at the counter and bent over to take a look at an all-too-familiar-looking pitcher.

I swallowed. Beads of sweat broke out on my forehead. "Nathan?" I burped. "I think I just drank your sea monkeys."

Thursday, June 24
Roll, Roll, Roll Your Goat

. . . .

"YOU DRANK MY SCIENCE experiment?" Nathan's voice wavered. Then he laughed. "That's so awesome!"

"I think I'm gonna be sick." I placed my hand over my mouth and sank to the floor. I hugged my knees and glanced up at Nathan.

He lifted the pitcher in the air and searched for survivors. "Maybe there's enough left to still do the experiment."

"Am I going to die?" I whimpered.

Nathan rolled his eyes. "Don't be a dork. They're just shrimp—think of it as eating sushi. Only you *drank* it instead." He laughed.

"I'm really sorry, Nathan." I slowly stood and leaned against the office doorway. "I didn't know there were sea monkeys swimming around inside. I thought you said they ate hard-boiled eggs—there aren't any egg bits floating around! You should have a sign on it or something." I didn't know what else to say.

"There aren't any egg bits because I remove the uneaten pieces each night. It'd stink otherwise. Of course, had I known you were going to drink it, I would've left some egg in there as a warning." He snorted again.

There was no way in the world Nathan would ever like me now. In his eyes, I'd always be the girl who ingested his science experiment. He'd probably want nothing to do with me.

"Do you want me to go with you back to the science lab and talk to Dave?" I asked. "I'll tell him what I did, that it's my fault."

Nathan shook his head. "Nah. I'll tell him—he's got more anyway. I just hope there's enough time for me to redo the experiment." He bent over to examine the pitcher once more. He looked at me. "So, how'd they taste?"

I punched him in the arm.

Nathan grabbed a sheet of paper from Cook's office and wrote, "DO NOT DRINK," on it. He taped it to the pitcher and headed back to the lab.

I wanted to go back to the cabin and just forget the whole day, but I still needed to bring Ms. Jacqueline her frosting. I searched the kitchen for the dolly but couldn't find it anywhere. Earlier, I had noticed a wagon near the trash cans next to the storage shed out back—that'd work. I might look dorky pulling a wagon full of frosting, but there was no other way to get something that heavy down the steep hill to the cake decorating kitchen. Taking a deep breath, I heaved the tub onto my hip and kicked the back door open with my foot. I felt my way down the three steps leading to the dirt path.

The wagon was next to the trash cans for an obvious reason. At a closer look, it was more rust than anything. I carefully lowered the frosting into the wagon. If I stuck to the sidewalk, it would be a smoother ride and the wagon *might not* rattle into a pile of rust dust before I got to the bottom.

I leaned over to grab the handle and realized I was still wearing the dish-washing apron. I took it off and tried to enter through the back door, but it had somehow locked behind me. I'd have to go in through the front of the mess hall.

I rounded the corner and came face-to-face with King Arthur.

Perfect. Pogo couldn't finish that tracking device soon enough.

I was not in the mood to deal with him. My patience for the goat was tinier than Nathan's sea monkeys.

Indiana Jones knew what he was doing traveling everywhere with a whip—he never knew when he'd need it, but he had it when he was in trouble. I needed to start traveling with a lead rope and halter. Only right now, all I had was the dish-washing apron.

I inched forward, holding the apron in front of me. If I could slip it around King Arthur's neck, it could work as a leash to haul him back to the barn.

"C'mon, man. I'm the one who saved you from the lake, remember?"

"Naa."

King Arthur galloped forward and leaped over the tub of frosting, clipping it with his hind legs. I scurried backward as the lid flew off and the tub toppled out of the wagon. King Arthur was undeterred. Squealing, I threw the rubber apron at him. It landed on his head, but he still kept charging. He looked like a superhero with his yellow cape of justice flapping in the breeze—only, in reality, he was a maniacal goat wearing a dishwasher's apron. As his head rammed into my leg, I desperately reached for anything to hold on to to keep from falling backward down Mess Hall Hill. The only thing I could reach was…King Arthur.

If I'm going down, you're going down with me. I grabbed hold as we tumbled head-over-hoof down the steep hillside in an alternating pattern.

Goat.

Apron.

Human.

Goat.

Apron.

Human.

That is, until the half-empty tub of chocolate frosting lost the battle to gravity at the top of the slope and caught up with us in our rapid tumble down Mess Hall Hill.

Goat.

Apron.

Human.

Chocolate frosting.

Goat.

Apron.

Human.

Chocolate frosting.

When we finally rolled to a stop, we were a mixture of chocolate frosting, grass, dirt, and goat hair.

I was so dizzy I was seeing double. Two goats stood and shook themselves. They simultaneously wobbled around for a few seconds, then trotted off, still wearing my dishwashing apron. I wasn't sure which goat was the real King Arthur. Apparently, his work here was done. He had succeeded in knocking me down the steepest hill at Camp Minnehaha.

Granted, I don't think he intended to go down it himself, but a victory is a victory.

I pushed myself to a sitting position as Ms. Jacqueline and the *whole* cake decorating class poured out the door and dashed to where I sat, spitting out blades of chocolate-flavored grass. I was covered with frosting from my head to my toes, smelled like a goat, and my stomach was churning—although that could've been because of the sea monkeys. I sat there. I wasn't sure what else to do. There was a rumbling in my ears that I attributed to the fall, but then, three seconds later, the wagon shot past me, crashed into a pine tree, and disintegrated into a mushroom cloud of rust dust.

I tried to drown my sorrows in an extra helping of banana pudding for dessert that night. When that didn't work, Pogo suggested a game of War during evening free time. We sat on my bunk and Pogo took my jack, king, and a ten in a single battle.

Sighing, I tossed my cards down in disgust. "This whole day sucks. How ironic is it that the one animal I hate is the one I'm stuck with?" I said. "That goat is a total moron."

Pogo looked sympathetically at me and laid down

another card. "I bet you'll feel better about the whole thing tomorrow. You're probably just tired and, dare I say, a little grumpy." She raised her eyebrow at me.

"Ever since King Arthur destroyed Mr. Snuffles, I've had a hard time falling asleep. I think it's because the plastic bag makes too much noise." I shook my head with a slight smile. "That sounds so pathetic—even to me."

Pogo nodded but grinned. "Wait here," she said and scurried to her top bunk. Seconds later, she was back with a paper bag. She reached in and pulled out...Mr. Snuffles?

A hand-sewn chef's hat covered the gaping hole in Mr. Snuffles's head and ear. Instead of a chewed-up T-shirt, he wore a small apron. His little gray body had been sewn up and restuffed. Gone were the dirt and slobber stains, and in his now-slightly-shorter trunk, he held a miniature wooden spoon. More than ever, he reminded me of Grandpa and the times we cooked together.

It was love at first sight.

I plucked Mr. Snuffles from her hand and held him close. "He's amazing! How did you do this?"

"I had to work fast. I grabbed him after lunch while you were on KP duty." Pogo giggled. "I was so afraid you'd come back to the cabin and notice he was missing and get even more upset!"

"But how did you sew him?"

"I took a sewing class a while back," Pogo said. "Ms. Jacqueline said I could use an old dish towel for fabric." She pointed to a line of stitches on Mr. Snuffles. "I used cotton balls to add stuffing and closed it up here. I figured a chef's hat was the perfect thing to cover the hole in his head since you like to bake."

"He's perfect." I gave Mr. Snuffles a big hug and kiss. "Thank you."

Thursday, June 24
8:52 p.m.

Pogo repaired Mr. Snuffles! He looks AWESOME!! I think she should've been awarded the Distinction of Recognized Kindness!! But it went to someone named Mark for teaching everyone in his cabin CPR.

On a totally separate note, today was officially Make Chloe Die of Embarrassment Day.

I drank Nath♥n's sea monkey experiment. At least he was a good sport about it. He is soooo sweet.

King Arthur escaped AGAIN, and this time he rammed me down Mess Hall Hill with a tub of frosting.

To make things even worse, when the cake decorating class dashed out to find me on the ground, covered in chocolate frosting, Victoria took the opportunity to snap a few photos on her phone. Rumor has it she asked Director Mudwimple if she could use the office printer to print out a cake design—yeah right! The next thing I know, photos of me with the words "Goat Girl" scrawled across them are plastered all over cabin doors and pine trees!!

According to Nath♡n, the pictures are even in the boy's bathroom in the mess hall!

My humiliation is complete.

Of course, Victoria denied it. She even showed Director Mudwimple her cake printout (like that's some form of proof of her innocence or something), but I know she did it.

She's had it out for me since day one.

And so has the stupid goat! Why should he hate me so much? It seems every time I turn around, King Arthur is following me—or ramming me down a hill or something. Doc thinks King Arthur likes my scent. He said goats have a terrific sense of smell and hearing. It's even been proven that goats can remember people for over a year, maybe even longer.

Then Doc said something HYSTERICAL. He said, "If you come back next year, he'll remember you." Like I would EVER come back here!!!!

The good news is, I'm finally finished with kitchen patrol duty. I bet this was the first time Victoria ever washed dishes—her chef probably does them at home. Must be nice.

Friday, June 25
Swallow Some Shower Gel

• • • • • • • • • • • • • • • • • • •

"Rabies!" screeched Victoria. "The goat has rabies!"

I shot up in bed. Where was I? Why was Victoria screaming? What goat?

King Arthur stood in the bathroom doorway. His four legs were spread wide and foam dripped from his mouth. His eyes were glazed over and he didn't look so hot.

"Where's Mindy?" I said.

"She's not here," Leslie squealed. "She had a meeting this morning!"

Sunlight was just beginning to pour through the cabin windows and our door stood open.

"She must not have pulled the door tight behind her," I said, swinging my feet out of bed. "Quick! Shut the cabin door, so he won't escape!"

"No way!" Marcie said. "Get him out!"

"We can't just have him running loose! Again." Pogo jumped down from her bunk.

Charlotte pushed the door shut with her foot. "Now what?"

"Catch him!" Victoria bounced on her knees on the top bunk. "Before he bites me."

"If you want him so bad, *you* come down and get him," I said.

King Arthur belched, spewing a waterfall of foam.

"Oh, gross!" Marcie scurried up to a top bunk.

"Poor guy," I said. "We gotta get him to Doc."

"Here." Pogo thrust her bathrobe belt into my hand. "Use this for a leash."

I walked toward King Arthur. "Here, boy…come here," I coaxed.

King Arthur shook his head, spraying slobbery bubbles in every direction.

Charlotte squealed, Ruth cried, and Leslie sat shaking on her top bunk in the corner, as far away from the action as she could get.

I let out a huff of disgust and walked toward him again.

King Arthur kicked out his back legs and charged. I yelped and jumped out of the way as he galloped toward the center of the cabin, leaving a trail of foamy bubbles.

He jumped onto a lower bunk. His eyes looked crazed

and foam was flying everywhere. He bounced from the bed to the floor and zoomed around and around, transforming our cabin into his personal racetrack.

"Look! The rabies must be getting worse," Anna said. "The bubbles are changing colors!"

Sure enough, the foam had turned pink and was becoming darker by the second.

He tried to make a tight turn, and his legs slipped out from underneath him. He stood and then stumbled. The foam was bright red now.

"Oh no," I said. "He's dying."

But instead of kicking the bucket, King Arthur wobbled over to the far corner, steadied himself, then barfed… right into Victoria's suitcase.

"Nooooooo!" Victoria wailed.

The unexpected, sweet smell of strawberries filled the cabin as a flood of multicolored bubbles and bright-pink gel erupted from his mouth.

Marcie's jaw dropped.

Charlotte's hand flew to her face.

Anna's eyes almost popped out of her head.

Pogo grabbed my arm in shock.

King Arthur dropped to his knobby knees and rested his head on the floor. I was no vet, but even I could tell he didn't feel good. I rushed over to him and slipped Pogo's bathrobe belt through his collar.

"That stupid goat!" Victoria screeched, climbing down from the top bunk.

"That puke looks and smells an awful lot like *your* shower gel!" I said, rubbing his neck to soothe him. "You know you're supposed to put your stuff away each night."

She stared blankly at me and then ran to the bathroom. A shriek vibrated the cabin windows.

She emerged from the bathroom moments later, clutching the empty, mangled bottle of her expensive shower gel. I waited for her to spontaneously combust in a fury-filled ball of fire as we giggled. "Losers," she hissed. "You're all losers. How dare you laugh at me!" Her eyes were wild with anger. "And my luggage! You're all a bunch of—"

"Enough!" Pogo stepped forward. "All you've done since the moment you arrived is treat us like dirt." Her hands clenched into fists. "I'm sick of it! If you want to talk to us like that, fine. But we don't have to stay here and listen." She turned around. "Come on, girls. Let's take King Arthur back to the barn and have Doc Mulholland check him out."

Victoria gaped as we walked out the door, all of us still in our pajamas—even Anna came. I led the way with King Arthur on the bathrobe leash. I know Victoria deserved everything she got—vomit and all—but I couldn't help feeling at least a teensy bit sorry she had such a gross mess to clean up. It was nasty.

Doc was already in the barn when we arrived. He raised an eyebrow in amusement when I handed him King Arthur's bathrobe leash. I started telling him what happened, and his expression changed to concern. He removed the stethoscope from around his neck and knelt beside King Arthur...who belched.

We all huddled in our jammies in a group as Doc listened to the goat's heart.

"Is he going to be okay?" I asked Doc. "He looks so pathetic."

Doc didn't answer right away but moved the stethoscope from King Arthur's heart to his belly. After a few minutes, he stood. "He'll be fine. He has a stomach of iron." He patted King Arthur's head. "Serves him right for eating stuff he shouldn't."

"That goat spends more time out of his stall than he does in it," I muttered.

Doc shut the stall door and double-checked the latch. He leaned over the top and rubbed one of King Arthur's ears. "Stay here, you rascal, understand?"

The goat belched again and a bubble floated out and up toward the rafters. I swear, King Arthur looked ashamed.

"Will he still be blowing bubbles when I show him to my parents tomorrow?" I asked.

Doc laughed. "No. I think most of the shower gel is out of his system. He might still smell like strawberries though."

"I'm cool with that—strawberries smell a lot better than goats."

He led us out of the barn. "Y'all get changed and grab some breakfast before they stop serving."

Victoria and her vomit-filled luggage were nowhere to be seen when we returned to get dressed.

"I wonder where Victoria went," said Pogo.

I shrugged. "I'm just glad she took the suitcase out of here. That is not something I want to see or smell right before I eat."

Our whole cabin, minus Victoria, sat together for breakfast for the first time, which was kind of sad. We had finally gotten close and camp was practically over.

Mindy and Director Mudwimple came over and joined us.

"I understand there was a bit of a catastrophe in the cabin this morning," Director Mudwimple said.

Charlotte told her everything.

Mindy held her hand over her mouth as though she was trying not to laugh. "I didn't want to wake you girls, so I gently shut the door. I guess I should've pulled a little harder—I am so sorry."

"No complaints here," I said.

Director Mudwimple raised her eyebrow at my comment.

"I *mean* because King Arthur's going to be okay, of course."

"Hmm," Director Mudwimple murmured, but she smiled.

I looked around for Victoria and didn't see her. "Where's Victoria?"

"The morning's event proved to be a bit much for Victoria," Director Mudwimple said. "She's in the nurse's office resting with a cool compress. Once she's calmed down, I'll let her use the laundry facilities to wash her things." She tapped her chin as though deep in thought. "It might take several washes to get everything clean."

I felt a stab of guilt. "I don't know how he could've gotten out. I promise I locked his gate last night."

"Don't fret, dear," Director Mudwimple said. "Doc was in the barn early this morning and saw the whole thing. He came around the corner just in time to see King Arthur leap from his climbing platform right over the fence." She sighed. "By the time Doc ran outside, King Arthur was long gone. Maybe that's been King Arthur's trick to escape these past few days. Doc has since moved him to another stall with no climbing structure."

That *might* explain how he was roaming free on the first day of camp and the incident with the frosting, but I seriously doubted King Arthur had jumped his pen the day of poor Mr. Snuffles's demise. I think he had help from Victoria.

Friday, June 25
Presume Everything Will Be Fine

. . . .

I MET POGO IN the science lab just before lunch. She wanted me to bring her one of King Arthur's collars, so she could attach the tracking device to it.

"Here's the collar," I said, setting it down. Her work-station was covered with colored wires, pliers, and bits and pieces of what I think used to be a cell phone. I raised my eyebrows in surprise.

Pogo laughed when she saw my expression. "Don't worry—that's all from my *old* cell phone."

"You brought both your old and new phone to camp?"

"I didn't mean to bring my old one. My little brother was playing with it on the car ride up here and must have stuck it in my bag. I discovered it when I unpacked—he's always putting stuff in my schoolbag. Last year, he shoved his Darth Vader action figure in with my pencils. Each time I reached for a pencil, Darth Vader would say, 'You underes-timate the power of the Dark Side.'" Pogo picked up a small box that had various wires and techy stuff attached to it and held it up to the collar.

"Is that the tracking device?"

"Yeah. I've been working on it like crazy. I found a free tracking app. I just need to link it to a sim card from my old phone. Then, I can load the app onto my new phone." She set it down.

"You'll be able to show your dad that you've put your daddy-daughter dates in the garage to good use."

She smiled. "*If* I can get it working in time."

"I bet you will—according to Sebastian, you're pretty smart." I winked.

She blushed. "C'mon. Let's get some lunch."

We walked toward the mess hall. In the distance, I could see large, gray clouds gathering. The air was thick with humidity and the wind had picked up. Rain was holding off, but I could tell it would pour at some point that day. I was actually looking forward to the storm—the rain would hopefully bring down the photos of me plastered all over the camp.

Garlic smells from the mess hall mixed with the scent of detergent as we passed by the laundry building. The door was open. Victoria wore rubber gloves and one of those masks that doctors wear on TV shows as she hosed out her suitcase. I figured the nurse gave it to her to use. An extra-large *Camp Minnehaha Rocks!* T-shirt hung down to her knees, and a pair of athletic shorts showed beneath.

"Wow," Pogo said under her breath. "I bet those clothes aren't what she's used to wearing."

"All her things are in the wash, I guess." I stole another look. "It looks like she had to scavenge the lost and found for something to wear." I nudged Pogo in the side. "I can't help but think King Arthur is good for something after all."

Pogo let out a laugh.

Victoria's head shot up at the sound of Pogo's laughter. She glared.

I returned to the barn after lunch to bathe King Arthur, who had fully recovered from his breakfast à la shower gel. Doc wanted all the animals groomed for the parent preview tomorrow. (I was the only camper whose animal had been soaped up both inside and out.)

After toweling him dry, I brushed his white, hairy coat until my arms ached. That goat never looked or smelled so good. While I polished his horns with horse hoof polish Doc gave me, King Arthur nibbled at my shoelaces. I danced my feet around, but he chased them like a kitten. I laughed and gently pushed him away. Dumb goat.

After his bath, he spent the rest of the afternoon secured

in his paddock. I tackled the stink of King Arthur's stall one last time. Cleaning his pen was toward the top of my list of many things I was not going to miss when camp ended. A three-day-old rotted cheeseburger smelled better than his stall. My eyes watered each time I plopped a shovel full of sopping, stinking wood shavings into the wheelbarrow.

I was almost done when Pogo sprang through King Arthur's door.

"I did it! I got it to work!" She thrust a collar toward me with the small box secured to it. Then she wrinkled her nose. "Man! What a smell."

"You're telling me," I said.

She pranced into the paddock and knelt next to King Arthur, who nibbled away at the grass. She fastened the collar around him, yanked her phone from her pocket, and pulled up the tracking app. "This will track him in real time, so you'll know right where he is," she called over her shoulder.

My final scoop of poop plopped into the wheelbarrow. "Great! Even if he does run off before my parents see him, I can find him now."

Doc popped his head around the stall door. "Hi, Paulie." His eyes lit up when he saw the collar and Pogo's phone. "Did you get it to work?"

"Yep, gone are his days of disappearing."

I grabbed a bag of clean wood shavings, emptied it into the stall, and started raking the shavings out to make a soft, sweet-smelling covering across the floor—a bed fit for a king.

Doc joined Pogo in the paddock and bent down to examine King Arthur's collar. "Oh, I'm sure he'll still disappear. We'll just know where he's disappeared to." He rubbed behind King Arthur's ear and gave him a pat on the head. "Don't tell the other animals, but this little guy is my favorite."

I looked up from raking. "Why?"

Doc laughed. "When I was a kid, my dad was prone to seizures and blackouts. My mom read an article about goats helping a lady with her seizures, so they got a couple for my dad. The goats could sense when he was about to have one, and they'd circle around him. He'd then go lie down, so he wouldn't bump his head. My dad called the girl Daisy, and I got to name the boy. I chose Roger."

I stifled a laugh. "Roger?"

"That doesn't really sound like a goat name," said Pogo.

A gust of wind swept through the barn, creating little dust tornadoes.

Doc nodded. "I know, but that's what I wanted to name a dog, so that's what the goat got. And he followed me everywhere and even came when I called. He was very affectionate and playful—just like a dog."

"So King Arthur's your favorite because he reminds you of Roger?" Pogo said.

"Yeah—but he also reminds me of my dad." He looked sad. "He died last year." Doc gave King Arthur one more pat on the head and stood. "I know this little guy's been a bit of a rascal for you."

A jarring crash of thunder ricocheted throughout the barn. I jumped.

Thud. King Arthur passed out in the grass.

I rolled my eyes. "Does he always faint when there's a thunderstorm?"

Doc laughed. "Most goats don't spook too easily with thunderstorms. In fact, some racehorse owners will keep goats to calm the horses during storms. Don't know how it works, but it does. His Highness, however, has a particular dislike of storms."

King Arthur stood and bleated, as though in agreement with Doc.

Pogo checked her phone. "I need to go back and make a few adjustments so it will work with the camp's equipment after I leave. Plus, the battery needs charging." She removed King Arthur's collar. "I'll be back in a little bit."

"But it's almost dinnertime," I said, pushing the wheelbarrow toward the door. Tonight was my lesson with Ms.

Jacqueline, and as much as I wanted the collar on my renegade goat, I couldn't risk being late.

"It shouldn't take too long," Pogo said. She walked out with Doc. "Just grab a tray for me and save a seat next to you. I'll be there before dinner's over—don't worry."

I brought King Arthur back into the stall, knelt down beside him, and scratched behind his ears while he nestled into the clean wood shavings. He gently nibbled at my free hand. I was surprised at how soft his lips felt. I rubbed his nose and then gave him a hug.

"You know," I said quietly, "I don't think you *mean* to be rotten. You just can't help yourself." I sat, leaning against the stall wall. He rested his head on my lap, and I continued rubbing his ears. The little guy was growing on me. "You're like a black hole of catastrophe and whoever happens to be near you gets sucked into it." I remembered Nathan's sea monkeys and how catastrophically stupid I had been when I drank them. But Nathan had forgiven me. I could maybe forgive King Arthur for eating Mr. Snuffles…and tipping my canoe…and ramming me down a hill…maybe one day.

I gave him a final pat on the head and stood. "You'll be safe in your stall during the storm, so don't go out tonight, okay, buddy?"

He blinked, and I took that to mean, *Yeah, sure.*

Outside, ominous storm clouds were piled high, and the sky was darker than normal for early evening. Raindrops were just starting to pelt me as I raced across the path and up the steps to the mess hall. A bright rip of lightning was followed closely by another crash of thunder filling the air. Nathan and Sebastian stood on the front porch.

"Aww, man! We gotta walk through that?" Nathan said.

"Where are you going?" I asked.

"We gotta get back to the science lab—we aren't done with our projects yet. We chowed through dinner in record time. Finished in under five minutes," Nathan said.

Sebastian shook his head. "No, no, we finished in under four—I timed us."

"Either way, you two are in for a nice, big helping of indigestion," I said. "Good luck with your projects, and I hope Dave has some Pepto-Bismol in the lab. See ya!"

I loaded up two trays—one for Pogo—and sat down. I'd just crammed a forkful of spaghetti into my mouth when Pogo ran into the mess hall looking scared.

"King Arthur's gone!"

Friday, June 25
Sacrifice a Dream

. . . .

WATER STREAMED FROM POGO'S hair and pooled on the floor. "I went to the barn to put his collar back on and he wasn't there. And I can't find Doc."

Another crash of thunder reverberated through the mess hall.

"Maybe Doc and King Arthur are together," I said hopefully.

Pogo shook her head and sent a spray of water over the table. "No, he said King Arthur would be in his pen so that I could put the collar back on him."

My lesson with Ms. Jacqueline was scheduled to start in just a few minutes. Her words, "It is the only time I have. You mustn't be late," ping-ponged around my head.

"He's an animal," I said. "They're okay in the rain. He'll find shelter."

Pogo gave me a disappointed look.

I gave her a glare.

Great. He had to get out tonight of all nights. Now I wasn't going to learn how to decorate cupcakes, and I wasn't going to be able to work for Mrs. Peghiny, and I wasn't going to be able to earn money to buy a new bike. All because of that stupid goat.

Something hit the roof of the mess hall.

A tree branch?

King Arthur was alone in the storm—and probably frightened. He was my responsibility even if he was a stupid goat, and he could get hurt.

I groaned. Why did that goat never listen to me?

"Let's go," I said.

Rain drenched my hair the moment I sprinted down the mess hall steps. A thunderous boom shook the windows behind us. Even though it was summer, the wind felt cold. The sky had grown even darker. It wasn't pitch-black, but I wished I had my flashlight.

We raced back to the barn. I held a tiny hope that Pogo was wrong. Maybe she had overlooked him. After all, Doc had moved King Arthur to a different stall.

"Doc!" Pogo said. "Are you here?"

I ran past every stall, checking for King Arthur.

Horse.

Horse.

Horse.

Llama.

Horse.

Cow.

No goat.

"Where should we look?" Pogo asked.

"Let's split up." I motioned to the tracking collar Pogo held in her hand. "That works, right?"

"Unless the storm has taken out the cell towers."

"We'll chance it." I grabbed it from her and put it on myself like a necklace. "This way at least we won't lose each other. If I find him, I'll stay put and you come to us. If you find him, you come get me. Got it?"

"Got it."

"I'll check around the mess hall, the cake kitchen, and the lake. You take the area near the cabins, the sports field, and science lab," I said as we headed out.

Pogo disappeared into the storm.

A gust of wind sprayed me with leaves and rain, and the dirt trail to the mess hall had transformed into a muddy glop.

I dashed around to Mess Hall Hill. A flash of lightning spiderwebbed across the sky. Trees waved back and forth in the wind, and I prayed a tornado wasn't coming. The wind was blowing the rain horizontally now, and the camp speakers sounded the alarm for bad weather. I didn't care—I had to find King Arthur.

I slipped and slid down the steep drop toward the cake kitchen and lake. Canoes rocked back and forth in the water. Weird. The canoes were always beached on the sand at the end of each day. Why were they in the water? Unless…

I remembered Director Mudwimple said something the first day of camp about the creek bed normally being real low…unless it stormed. All the watershed from Mess Hall Hill would funnel down the ravine and fill the creek. The creek water drained into the lake. If the canoes were floating, it was because the ravine was filling with water.

I sprinted toward the sidewalk leading up to the mess hall. Another flash of lightning gave me a momentary view of the hilltop. Someone was up there, but who?

Then, through the downpour, I spied Victoria gripping a paisley umbrella that had been blown inside out by the wind.

She dodged around the corner of the mess hall. What was she doing? No one would be out in this storm unless they absolutely had to be.

I followed her as she darted behind the storage shed. The wooden fence that separated level ground from the ravine drop-off seemed to be her target. She knelt by a post.

"What are you doing out here?" I hollered as I ran up to her.

Victoria held a chewed lead rope in one hand. The other end was looped over the top of the fence post.

"I don't understand. He's supposed to be right here," she stammered. "This is where I—"

A crash of thunder drowned out the rest of her words.

"What have you done?"

Her face had gone white. "This is where I left him."

Friday, June 25
Get Stuck between a Rock and a Hard Place

· · · · · · · · · · · · · · · · · · · ·

"You took King Arthur from his stall? He's terrified of storms!" I said.

She started blathering on. I could barely hear her over the storm "…everyone stays away from the ravine…I figured…good place to hide him."

"The ravine!" What if he fell into the ravine?

Thunder crashed around us. Victoria jumped and grabbed my arm.

I shook her off and ran toward the ravine. The normally dry streambed was filling with the runoff. Branches and leaves raced toward Lake Minnehaha.

Another flash of lightning in the black sky revealed something white in the water.

King Arthur.

He stood in the middle of the river, leaning against a boulder. The water was at his knees, moving fast and rising. The boulder was the only thing keeping him from being swept away. I couldn't hear him over the sound of the pouring rain or thunder, but I saw his small mouth open and shut, bleating for help. If he fainted, he might drown before I could get to him.

I turned to Victoria. "There's a rescue ring with a throw line down at the pier. Hurry!"

Victoria ran toward the lake and I slid down the steep slope of the ravine and into the muddy river. It came up to midcalf on me, and with King Arthur's small frame, it would soon be deadly. The current was powerful and I struggled to keep my feet under me.

"It's okay, buddy," I called to him. "Just keep your head up. I'm coming for you."

There was a huge thunderclap, and that was all he could take. He fainted.

I grabbed him as he slipped under. Trying to lift him up higher, I gave him a tug, but he was stuck. I plunged my arm into the water and felt a large rock wedging one of his legs against the boulder.

King Arthur shook his head and began bleating like crazy.

I tried to pick the rock up but couldn't. It was too hard to keep hold of the goat and reach down into swift water. The current kept threatening to push me over.

I searched the top of the ravine.

Where was Victoria?

King Arthur frantically reared up.

I jumped back, away from his horns. "Easy, boy."

A floating branch smacked the back of my calf. I grabbed it and shoved it into the water and under the rock and pushed down. The rock moved...but then—

The branch snapped.

"No!" I screamed, and I hurled the top part of the branch away. I grasped the shorter piece that was still wedged under the rock and tried again, pushing with all my strength. Cold water swirled around my fingers. King Arthur jerked his head up, and the tip of a horn smacked me in the mouth.

Ouch! I let go of the branch and grabbed my mouth. I tasted blood.

The water was now at his neck.

I didn't have much time.

Tears mixed with rain on my face. "We can do this, buddy." I rubbed his head. "I'm going to push on that stick and you have to pull your leg out."

"I'm back," Victoria hollered. She held up the rescue ring. It was attached to several yards of throw line.

"Tie the end around that tree." I pointed.

She tied it off and threw me the ring.

I caught it and slipped my head and one arm through it. "Come and help me push down on this stick! We've got to free his leg!"

She looked wide-eyed at the river and shook her head.

"Please, Victoria! Just hold on to the rope." I begged. "I can't do it by myself!"

King Arthur bleated.

Victoria looked at him, and gripping the rope for dear life, she stepped into the water.

I turned back to King Arthur. "Okay, buddy, we're getting you outta here. But I'm going to need your help too. Doc told me you're supersmart, so I'm going to give some instructions I need you to follow. I'm going to try once more to lift this rock, and when I do, you gotta move your leg. Otherwise, you won't be around to ram any more campers." My voice broke. We had to save him.

Victoria made it out to us.

"I've got part of the stick jammed under the rock that's trapping him. We gotta push down on it at the same time," I said.

She nodded and placed her hands next to mine.

I looked at her. "One…two…three!"

The branch shook as our combined weight pushed down on it. I prayed it wouldn't break.

Suddenly the rock shifted and King Arthur's leg jerked up.

"We did it!" Victoria yelled.

I wrapped my arms around King Arthur. "I've got you." His heart threatened to beat right out of his chest.

Victoria tugged on my shoulder. "We got to get out of this water."

I nodded and wiggled the life ring down to my waist. "I'll hold him while you pull us."

Victoria pulled her way back to shore with the rope. Then she began tugging us in.

It wasn't easy with rushing water trying to sweep my feet out from under me and a terrified goat wiggling in my arms.

I slipped as I scrambled up the muddy bank but rolled to the side so I wouldn't squish King Arthur. Victoria dropped the rope and fell down next to us.

In the darkness, covered in mud, leaves, and twigs, I lay on the bank, next to King Arthur and Victoria. We were all three exhausted.

After a couple moments, I realized that the rain had become a steady sprinkle instead of a downpour, and the thunder had stopped. I rubbed King Arthur's head and plucked a wet leaf off one of his horns. "If he could talk, he'd probably apologize for the vomit in your suitcase this morning."

Victoria let out a small laugh.

I pulled the tracking collar off my neck, hoping it

hadn't gotten ruined by the water, and put it around King Arthur's neck, where it belonged.

"I'll go up to the mess hall. Maybe someone's there who can help us," Victoria said.

"I'll stay with King Arthur."

I leaned back next to him. His body quivered. I didn't know if it was because he was cold or scared. I held his face in my hands. "You're filthy," I said. "All that time grooming you? Down the tubes—or down the river in this case." I rubbed his nose. "Oh well. I'd rather show Mom and Dad a dirty goat than a dead one."

He nibbled the life ring.

I glanced after Victoria. How many other times had she let him out? More than once. Of that I was positive.

A powerful beam of light blinded me.

"Chloe!"

I stood and waved. "We're over here!" I yelled. "King Arthur's hurt!"

Two beams of light jostled down to where I stood— Pogo and Director Mudwimple holding flashlights.

Mudwimple squeezed any river water I had in me out with her strong hug. "Oh, dear heart, we've found you! You had us frightened to death."

Doc and Ms. Jacqueline and Victoria ran up.

I pointed to King Arthur. "His leg is hurt."

"What happened?" Doc asked, bending down to examine Arthur's leg.

I looked at Victoria. She stared at the ground and hunched her shoulders like she was trying to become invisible. *Way to claim it, Victoria.*

I sighed. "He was wedged between that boulder and a rock." I knelt beside Doc, who was running his hands over King Arthur. "Will he be okay?"

"I don't feel any broken bones. And he's acting normal." Doc pointed to the life ring King Arthur was snacking away on. "But I'll want to do a thorough examination back at the barn."

I saw a bloody bandage taped to Doc's forehead when he stood. "What happened to your head, Doc?"

"A gust of wind and the paddock door. It looks worse than it is."

Ms. Jacqueline held Doc's hand and moved in closer to him.

"I found him," Pogo said. "And helped him to the nurse's cabin. While we were there, I noticed your signal wasn't moving." She waved the phone at me. "Figured you'd found King Arthur. So we headed over this way and Victoria waved us down."

Director Mudwimple draped one chubby arm across

my shoulders and another across Victoria's and she pulled us in. "I am so glad you girls are safe."

Then she leaned over and scooped King Arthur up. "This guy can catch a ride back to the barn with us in the golf cart."

Friday, June 25
Make a Truce

. . . .

KING ARTHUR, POGO, AND I sat in the back of the mega-golf cart. Victoria rode up front with Director Mudwimple, talking about who knows what. Doc and Ms. Jacqueline held hands and leaned against each other in the middle seats. We dropped the two lovebirds off at the nurse's station, and Director Mudwimple let Victoria get out at our cabin. Then the rest of us headed for the barn.

Once there, Director Mudwimple and I added extra wood shavings for King Arthur to sleep on, while Pogo secured any doors, gates, mouse holes, or cracks that he might possibly get through. I was confident he wouldn't be going anywhere though.

"Can I stay with him tonight?" I asked Director Mudwimple.

She chuckled and shook her head. "No, my dear. You need your sleep too. I know you're concerned about him, but he's fine." She pulled me in for another bear hug.

"Thank you for saving his life, but don't ever scare me like that again."

"I promise I won't," I said. "But only if he keeps his part of the bargain and doesn't go into any ravines during storms."

"Naaaa," bleated King Arthur.

"Are you agreeing with me?" I asked him.

I could've sworn I saw him wink.

Victoria was sitting on the porch steps when Director Mudwimple dropped Pogo and me off at the cabin.

I was surprised she wasn't inside, showering and using up all the hot water. My jaw tightened.

"I'm going inside," Pogo said, climbing the stairs. She pulled her shirt away from her body and took a whiff. "Whew! I need a shower."

"Catch ya later," I said.

I stood, waiting for Victoria to say something.

She held my stare but squirmed. I didn't care if she felt uncomfortable. Even though she helped rescue King Arthur, I was still pretty miffed she hadn't coughed up the truth back at the ravine.

She cleared her throat. "I didn't mean for King Arthur to get hurt. I just wanted you to be embarrassed—like I was this morning." She swiped a lock of wet hair behind her ear. "It'd be pretty bad if all you had to show your parents tomorrow was an empty stall." She sighed. "So I took him. Tomorrow I would have 'found' your missing goat and been the hero, *for once*. Then the storm got bad, so I figured I'd better put him back—but he'd eaten through the rope, obviously."

"Yeah, he does stuff like that." *But that's not news to you.*

Victoria stood. "Are you going to tell on me?"

"He could have died," I said.

"I know."

"But he didn't."

She gave me a nod. Truce.

Friday, June 25
9:26 p.m.

Holy cow—what a night!!
The whole camp could've seen me drenched with river water, covered in dirt and leaves, and clinging to a half-drowned goat tonight, and I WOULDN'T CARE!!!!!!

Because all that really matters is that King Arthur didn't die.

Even when Nath♥n saw King Arthur and me (with a busted lip) in the back of the golf cart soaking wet and dirty, it didn't bother me. Nath♥n looked concerned at first (because of my lip?), but then he laughed when he saw King Arthur—but it was more like a "Cool! The goat is riding in a golf cart" laugh.

If anyone had told me I'd be rescuing a goat alongside my sworn enemy, I'd tell them that octopuses have toes! I guess she's my ex-sworn enemy. I'm NOT SAYING we're friends—we've just more or less called a truce.

I feel a little sorry for Victoria. I know she's angry for always being compared to JT. She never gets to be a hero. She caused all the trouble tonight, but if she hadn't pulled herself together and helped me, King Arthur would have died. I guess that kind of makes her a hero.

Poor King Arthur—if Victoria comes back next year, I bet he'll faint from fear the minute he sees her!

Pogo is sooooo happy that her crazy, amazing tracking device worked! Her dad's gonna be amazed too, I bet!

I can't wait to show Mom and Dad the barn—and not just King Arthur but all the animals. I'll need to give His Highness another bath and brush him out before they see him, but's that's okay.

Good night—I'm exhausted!

PS Doc and Ms. Jacqueline are totally gaga for each other. It's pretty obvious.

PPS I'm pretty sure King Arthur has eaten more flotation devices than what's considered healthy—even for a goat.

PPPS My lip hurts—I hope it doesn't look too ugly in the morning!

Saturday, June 26
Try Not to Be a Dork

. . . .

AFTER BREAKFAST, EVERYONE WAS sent to their cabins to pack and clean (except for Victoria, who was washing dishes). I tried a million times to roll my sleeping bag in a tight cylinder like Dad always did, but it ended up looking like a telescope. I finally gave up and played checkers on the porch with Pogo while we kept an eye out for our parents.

Luckily, the swelling had gone down on my lip overnight, and with the help of a little of Charlotte's makeup, I actually looked good.

"Chloe!" Mom and Dad walked across the grass, holding hands.

I ran and wrapped my arms around them. "I missed you guys so much!"

Mom squeezed me tight and then held me out at arm's length. "Did you have fun?"

"Yep!"

"Let's get your stuff into the van and then you can show us all the cake-decorating stuff you learned," Dad said.

"Yeah, well, that didn't really work out. Not sure how I'm going to earn money for a bike now." I shrugged. "I'll have to come up with a new idea."

We tossed my stuff in the van, and I led them toward the barn.

"I ended up looking after King Arthur."

"King Arthur?" Dad asked.

"He's a goat—with issues."

Mom and Dad stopped dead in their tracks.

"You took care of an animal?" Dad said.

"Yep, and I actually enjoyed it—sort of—toward the end—the very end."

King Arthur, once again groomed and free of twigs and leaves, nibbled away at the mound of hay in the center of his stall. I fumbled with his door but got it open and ushered my parents through.

Dad gave him a pat on the head and Mom stroked his back.

"He seems sweet," she said. "Was he fun to take care of?"

Sure, if you like swimming in lakes, having precious belongings ingested, rolling down hills, and doing water rescues. King Arthur wandered over to me and gently nudged my leg, asking for a pet. I rubbed his ear. "It was definitely an experience I won't forget anytime soon."

Doc joined us inside the stall. "Mr. and Mrs. McCorkle?" He no longer had the bandage on, but a large lump with a nasty bruise covered the right side of his head.

"This is Doc Mulholland," I said. "He's the vet."

"Nice to meet you," Mom said.

Dad gestured toward Doc's head. "You and King Arthur have a head-butting competition?"

Doc laughed. "No, no, he'd win for sure if we did that. Just an accident from the storm last night—lost a battle with a swinging door. I wanted you to know that Chloe's been a *huge* help to all of us here at Minnehaha." He patted my shoulder and winked. "She's very responsible and extremely good with animals."

I *was* good with animals—which surprised even me. I'd never really liked them before, but maybe that was because I didn't know much about them. But being surrounded for the last two weeks by fur, fuzz, and feathers had gotten me used to them. Plus, with Doc's animal classes each day, I had learned a lot. Animals were actually kind of fun.

Then *the* idea popped into my head—the idea I'd been waiting for.

Pet-sitting.

Pet-sitting would solve my money problems! Maybe more people in the neighborhood were due to go on vacation—people with pets. I could practice all the stuff Doc had taught me—at least with cats and dogs. I was pretty sure there weren't a lot of people with cows, horses, or, thankfully, goats in my neighborhood.

Pet-sitting. My heart pounded with excitement at my idea. I had to time this right though. There was a good chance Mom and Dad would collapse on the barn floor in laughter once I shared my idea. I studied Mom and Dad. They were smiling. That was good sign. They were holding hands. Another good sign. They could support each other and not fall down in hysterics.

I cleared my throat. "So, Mom and Dad, after what Doc Mulholland said about me being responsible and good with animals," I said, "how about I start pet-sitting?"

They stayed upright. Seriously.

Dad raised his eyebrow and glanced at Mom.

"What do you think?" Dad asked.

I clasped my hands together. "Please?"

Dad's mouth twitched sideways, like he was considering my request. "Are you sure, Chloe? Are you ready to take on animals?"

"Yes! I want to try this, Dad. Please!"

Mom squeezed Dad's hand. "What about Napoleon?"

Dad nodded. "I think we're on the same page."

"Well?" I bounced on my toes.

"Actually, Mr. Philips is going on vacation for a week and needs someone to watch his dog," Dad said. "He mentioned it just this morning."

"Care to give it a shot?" Mom said. "It would be a good trial run."

I squealed. "Yes! I'll do it! Can I make flyers and hand them out around the neighborhood when we get back?"

"Let's see how it goes with Napoleon first," Dad said.

I wrapped my arms around them and squeezed. "Thank you!"

The dream of a new bike had returned.

"Oh! I almost forgot," I said. "Guess who else is here? Nathan and Sebastian, from school. They're in the science lab with Pogo. C'mon."

"Who's Pogo?" Dad asked.

"My friend."

We checked out the science fair and visited with Nathan's parents. Major Maddux, Nathan's dad, laughed so hard at the story of me drinking the sea monkeys that he started hiccupping—and that made *me* laugh.

"Let's just hope no one asks you to pet-sit any sea monkeys," Dad said.

The camp speakers crackled, and Director Mudwimple's voice came through. "Parents, I hope you are having a wonderful time seeing what our campers have been doing these past two weeks. It's now time for our banquet, complete with desserts made by our cake decorating class. Please make your way to the mess hall."

The mess hall looked like a fancy restaurant. White linen tablecloths covered each table, and there were more forks and spoons at each setting than I knew what to do with. The smells of garlic, butter, and various herbs made my stomach rumble. The food was at the far end of the mess hall.

We got our lunch and sat with Pogo and her family. Garlic-ginger green beans, potatoes au gratin, chicken stuffed with smoked Gouda and bacon, and some fancy bread I couldn't pronounce filled my plate.

Toward the end of the meal, Coach Fox stood on the stage and whistled for our attention.

"Ladies and gentleman," he bellowed. "Director Mudwimple has something to say."

Director Mudwimple climbed next to him and looked around. "We really enjoyed having all your kids here. They've decorated some amazing treats, cared for our precious animals, and the science group in particular has been quite inventive. And after observing the sports teams, I have no doubt that I'll be cheering on some of our campers in the NFL or NBA one day." She waited as parents applauded. "However, there are three campers in particular I want to say something about.

"Last night, we had a pretty bad storm here. I'm sure you noticed all the fallen branches and debris on the ground. A tornado went through several miles east of here." She stopped and took a deep breath, almost like she was getting choked up.

"In the middle of the storm, one of our animals—a goat named King Arthur—got out of his stall. Though I have to say the fact the King Arthur escaped is nothing new around here."

The mess hall filled with knowing murmurs and laughter from my fellow campers.

"If it hadn't been for the quick actions and excellent teamwork of three of our campers, Paulie Smithfield, Chloe McCorkle, and Victoria Radamoskovich, King Arthur might have died." She cleared her throat. "I would like to honor Victoria, Chloe, and Paulie with our Distinction of Recognized Kindness award. *If* they decide to return to Camp Minnehaha next summer, they may have first pick of any elective they choose."

What? Victoria got an award for almost killing the goat?

Across the hall, Victoria's mother was smiling and her father was looking at her like maybe he'd never seen her before. And Victoria was beaming from ear to ear. A real smile—not a smirk. Who knew that conceited, dissatisfied face of hers even knew how to smile?

She caught me looking at her and her smile was replaced by something else. Guilt? Fear?

I shook my head to tell her she didn't need to worry about me telling on her.

Dad crushed me in a hug then. "Proud of my girl," he whispered.

Director Mudwimple motioned us forward. "Ladies?"

Pogo and I started to weave our way through the tables to meet with Victoria up front. There was more applause, and some dorks in the back made bleating noises like a goat—I'm pretty sure it was Sebastian and Nathan.

Just as I made it to the front of the mess hall, I tripped and fell. My face burned with embarrassment. Sheesh. How was it I could run down a muddy ravine, keep my balance in a strong current, rescue a goat, help carry it uphill, and *not* fall over, but put me on a dry, flat floor in front of a couple hundred people and I fall flat on my face? As I picked myself up, I stole a look at Nathan.

He gave me a friendly smile.

I took a bow and everyone laughed. It felt good.

Director Mudwimple handed us certificates, and we hurried back to our seats—well, Pogo and I hurried. Victoria stayed up there longer, smiling and posing for everyone.

"Can I, Mom and Dad? Can I come back next summer?" I said, sitting back down.

"We'll see," Mom said, but she winked at Dad. That usually meant yes.

Dad leaned over to me. "Radamoskovich? Is she any relation to JT Radamoskovich?"

"His sister."

Dad scanned the mess hall, like he was checking to see if the football star was having lunch with everyone. "His quarterback sneak play is the best I've seen in a long time."

"Yeah? Must run in the family," I muttered. "Victoria has some sneaky moves of her own."

Pogo choked on her cupcake.

When the banquet ended, Pogo and I waddled our overstuffed bodies to the barn one more time to say good-bye to the animals. King Arthur was in his pen, quietly munching away at an afternoon snack. Did he ever *not* eat? I rubbed behind his ears, bent over, and gave him a big hug.

"Hope I see you next year, buddy."

He nudged me gently, as if to say, *Me too.*

Pogo draped her arm over my shoulder. "Someone needs to take care of that little guy."

I nodded. "Thanks for everything, Pogo."

She cocked her head. "Who's Pogo?"

I slapped my hand over my mouth. I couldn't believe I let the name slip out.

"It's my nickname for you," I said sheepishly. "I meant it as a compliment, 'cause you're always bouncing and bubbly."

She stared at the ground without talking.

"I'm sorry," I said. "I hope I didn't hurt—"

Her head shot up. "I like it! It's perky!"

We pulled out of the camp parking lot around five o'clock. I cradled Mr. Snuffles in my arms and watched as the landscape changed from forests to country fields to family neighborhoods. I pulled my journal out from the side pocket of my suitcase and opened it up.

Saturday, June 26
5:51 p.m.

Camp Minnehaha was AWE-SOME!

Doc Mulholland proposed to Ms. Jacqueline at the grand finale banquet—she said yes!!! IT WAS SOOOOO ROMANTIC!!!!!!!!

I saw Pogo and Sebastian take a photo together. And they traded phone numbers. I'm pretty sure Sebastian likes her.

Nath♥n has been supersweet to me this whole time. Before he left this afternoon, he came over and said good-bye. Then...he HUGGED me—sort of. It was more like a sideways hug. I wonder if that means he likes me—I hope so! I'm so glad he lives in my neighborhood and we can hang out more before school starts.

I have several weeks of summer vacation left, and I know just how I'm going to use them.

#1 Pet-sit like crazy.

#2 Save up money to buy a new bike (in turquoise, not pink).

#3 Convince my parents to let me and Mr. Snuffles go back to Camp Minnehaha next summer.

I totally just realized if you turn Distinction of Recognized Kindness into an acronym, it spells DORK!

LOL!!

I guess I don't mind being a dork after all!

Acknowledgments

· ·

I'd like to thank my husband David, for once again taking time to think things through with me on the front porch, while drinking tea. Here's to many more moments like that. You are my constant encourager, building me up each day, and demonstrating your love. I am blessed to be yours.

A special thanks to both Word Weavers and The Inkstigators. Charlotte, Anna, Ruth, Leslie, Marcea (Marcie)— y'all make great cabin mates, and despite what I wrote, y'all are the best!

Thank you Steve Geck for loving the story and helping me polish it to a shine.

And I want to give a big thank-you to Sally Apokedak of the Leslie H. Stobbe Literary Agency. No one could ask for a better agent! Thanks for your continuous hard work, encouragement, and dedication to the craft. You've made me a better writer and I look forward to learning even more from you.

About the Author

. . . .

Taryn's first book, *Whole-y Cow! Fractions Are Fun* was published by Sleeping Bear Press (2010), and Scholastic purchased paperback rights. It was a bestseller for Scholastic's Book Clubs in the nonfiction category in March 2011.

Her middle grade novel *Dead Possums Are Fair Game* was released by Sky Pony Press in November 2015.

Taryn graduated from the University of North Texas with a degree in Interdisciplinary Studies and a specialization in Mathematics. She taught middle school until she and her husband had kids. She now stays at home with her three children and volunteers at their schools.

Taryn is a member of both SCBWI and Word Weavers International. She currently lives in Winter Park, Florida with her husband, David, their three children, and two very fuzzy cats, Mordecai and Cyrus. Her website is www.TarynSouders.com.